SEEKING HAPPILY EVER AFTER

ELENA AITKEN

Also by Elena Aitken

Ever After

Choosing Happily Ever After

Needing Happily Ever After

Wanting Happily Ever After

Fighting Happily Ever After

We Wish You A Happily Ever After

Keeping Happily Ever After

Finding Happily Ever After

Seeking Happily Ever After

Cherishing Happily Ever After

Ever After: Volume One (Books 1-4)

The Springs Series

Summer of Change

Falling Into Forever

Second Glances

Winter's Burn

Midnight Springs

She's Making A List

Summit of Desire

Summit of Seduction

Summit of Passion

Fighting For Forever

Chapter One

THE CRY JOLTED Nick Newton awake from a dead sleep. He grappled around in the dark for his glasses, followed by his cell phone.

It was quarter past two.

Too early. *Way* too early.

He held his breath, hoping whatever had caused her cry was a one-off. A fluke. Maybe he'd dreamed it and—

Another ear-shattering scream, this one more insistent than the last, split the air.

No, he definitely hadn't imagined it.

With a shake of his head, he threw the quilt aside and crossed the room to the crib he'd set up in the corner. "Hey there, princess." He reached down, but stopped short to see Amelia, seven months old, standing in the crib, her chubby fists clamped around the rails of the wooden crib. "This is new." He smiled, marveling for a moment, even in his sleepy state, that she'd reached another milestone. It was the first time she'd pulled herself up in the crib. But the baby was in no mood for pleasantries. She cried out again, so Nick quickly gathered her up in his arms.

"What's this all about, kiddo?" He rocked her close. "Why are you awake? It's not a normal time of day. Daddy doesn't function at two a.m." If he hadn't been so exhausted, Nick would have laughed at himself. It wasn't that long ago that he was only getting the party started at two in the morning. Now, his party consisted of him, in a one-bedroom guest house, with a baby.

Things had changed.

Amelia had settled and was reaching up to his face with her chubby hands. He couldn't help but smile and bend down, offering his nose to be grabbed.

Yes, things certainly had changed. Absolutely everything had changed—for the better.

He yawned as Amelia's fingers clamped around his nose and squeezed.

Okay, maybe not everything had changed for the better. The lack of sleep he was still dealing with was definitely not an improvement.

At least before, when he was in the club partying, or entertaining a young lady or two in his fancy, overpriced penthouse until the sun came up, he could sleep well through the afternoon if he needed. And that was a very different type of exhaustion. Being the sole caregiver for a baby was next-level exhaustion. A bone-deep tired that never seemed to go away, no matter how much sleep he managed to get. Which, truthfully, was not much at all.

Just when he thought he had Amelia's schedule sorted out, she mixed it up on him.

"What do you need, princess? It's too early for breakfast, and…" He patted her bottom. The diaper was dry. He was too tired to think clearly, but if it wasn't the diaper, or hunger, then…what?

Nick shifted her in his arms and collapsed onto the couch in the guest house he was temporarily calling home. Amelia giggled. It was something she was doing more and more of lately, and he never tired of the noise. It was the sweetest thing he'd ever heard. To say that he was completely head over heels with the little girl would be a massive understatement. Never had another female had such an immense impact on him. Ever.

And that was saying something, considering for the last few years, since he and his best friend Damon Banks had sold their microchip design and had in turn become billionaires, Nick had turned into somewhat of a ladies' man. Which was a nice way of saying that, basically, he'd been sowing some wild oats and probably having too much fun. He'd had plenty of chances to meet *the one.*

Instead, he'd met the one who would make him a father.

Father.

The word still felt strange, even to think. Let alone to say aloud. Especially because despite his feelings for Amelia, and they were strong, he knew he wasn't her father. Not her biological one anyway. And that was going to be a problem. A big one.

If anyone found out.

It was something that occupied more and more of his thoughts over the last few weeks. Nick wasn't stupid; far from it. He rocked the baby, who'd finally lost interest in Nick's nose and was settling back into slumber, now content in his arms, and with his free hand, Nick pulled out his phone and clicked onto the file he'd received a few weeks earlier.

Jessica Silva.

It was all in there. Everything about Amelia's mother, the woman he'd dated—if you could even call a few hook-ups *dating*—over a year ago. Well over a year ago. Nick hadn't made his fortune being unsure about anything. He'd done the math. It didn't add up.

Amelia couldn't be his. Not biologically. He hadn't known

that when Jessica's sister, Lacy, had appeared at his friend's wedding six months ago and unceremoniously dumped the baby with him, declaring him the father. It hadn't been until the days and weeks after when he knew it with certainty and had begun the investigation into where exactly Jessica was and why she didn't want to be a mother.

He scrolled through the file his private investigator had provided him with, even though he already knew it by heart.

There was nothing positive in it. Drugs. Alcohol. A series of men. Crappy apartments.

Until very recently.

Jessica had a steady job now. She was clean. She'd rented a townhouse with a small yard, in a decent neighborhood.

All good signs that she was getting her life together.

Nick clicked the phone off and gazed down at the now sleeping baby. His heart swelled with a love he didn't even know was possible to feel until Amelia had been dropped into his life.

And now, he couldn't imagine his life without her. Which was why he couldn't stop thinking about how to make sure he never would have to.

Charlotte Davis clicked through the photos her mother, Darlene, had emailed her for the real estate listing they were working on. Dishes piled on the counter, with every type of appliance ever invented covering every inch of space. Dirty dishtowels hung from the oven and refrigerator door.

Terrible.

Char tried not to roll her eyes and even though her mother hadn't asked, she jotted down a few notes about how to make the space look more appealing. It wouldn't take much to trans-form the space. She couldn't completely tell from the photos, but it looked like the kitchen itself was pretty nice, with a classic white tile backsplash and granite countertops that should be showcased instead of cluttered up.

Her parents, Darlene and Dwayne Davis, had been Glacier Falls' top real estate agents, and had recently come back out of retirement to take advantage of the market that was starting to heat up. In their absence, things had changed. A lot.

Not only was Glacier Falls starting to become a hot spot for city folk who were desperate to escape the hustle and bustle and experience the beauty of the mountains and all that was offered with small-town living, but there was more competition between agents. Maybe Char didn't have much experience in real estate, but it didn't take an expert to see that the photos her mother had sent over were terrible, and were not going to help get top dollar for the house.

Charlotte sighed and dropped her chin to her chest in a quick neck stretch.

She was grateful her parents had offered her the job, to be sure. But working for her parents when she was thirty-two years old because she'd just had to move home to live with them after an epically failed relationship was not exactly where Charlotte thought she would be in her life at this point.

Not even close.

But it was better than the alternative. She still shuddered when she thought about the poor decision-making that had led her to a relationship with Billy Grant, the man she'd met with an online dating app. He'd seemed like a good guy, if not a little rough around the edges, when they'd first started talking online and then moved things to phone and video calls. He'd really cared about her and what she was interested in and what she was doing. He proclaimed his love early and often. All signs that, in hindsight, should have alerted her, but her judgment was off.

No. It was completely malfunctioning.

It made her so angry with herself to think about how she'd fallen for him and had ignored all the red flags that had been so apparent. She was smarter than that. Yet, when he'd asked her to move across the country to be with him, she hadn't even hesitated. She quit her interior design job with an up-and-coming home builder in the city, sold everything she owned, pushed away her family's concerns and had jumped on a plane to Halifax. Only three months later, it had become clear that Billy Grant was not the sweet, caring, happily ever after she'd dreamed he was.

He was a controlling narcissist who'd managed to, piece by piece, strip away her self-esteem and self-worth until she didn't even recognize herself. It wasn't until after Christmas when her parents came for a visit that she had begun to see for herself that the situation she was in wasn't healthy. Still, it had taken a few more weeks for Charlotte to get up the courage to call her brother Jeremy for help.

And now she was home.

She stretched her arms over her head and, opting to talk to her mom in person about the terrible photos, pushed up from the kitchen table that she was using for a temporary office. Her parents had recently moved into an office space just off Main Street, but working from home gave her a little bit of space from them, or at the very least, the illusion of space. She loved her parents, she really did, but it was not normal to be living at home at her age.

She really needed to find a little apartment or something and move out. Of course, to do that, she'd need more money.

Charlotte tried not to think about the circle she was caught up in and instead pulled a sweater over her head. Maybe a morning walk would help to clear her head on more than one level.

April in Glacier Falls was unpredictable. The town was positioned in the valley so that, despite being tucked in among some of the most beautiful mountain ranges in the world, warm winds blew in early to provide an earlier-than-expected spring season. But that didn't mean that they couldn't be treated to a freak snowstorm at any time.

The sun was shining and warm on her face as Charlotte took her time walking to the office. She stopped to investigate some of the community garden beds for signs of life and found tulips and daffodils pushing up through the soil. It wouldn't be long before everything was in bloom and the grass was green again. Spring was Charlotte's favorite time in Glacier Falls. It had been too long since she'd spent the season in her hometown.

Maybe there were some positives with having to return home?

The smell of freshly baked honey buns floated on the breeze and Charlotte straightened.

Yes. There were definitely positives to being back in Glacier Falls.

The bells over the bakery door jingled as she stepped inside. She shut her eyes and inhaled deeply. Nothing smelled as good as delectable aromas coming from the ovens in the back of Sweetie Pies.

"Oh, sorry."

Charlotte jostled and almost fell over as the door to the bakery opened directly into her back. She probably should have gotten out of the way. "No," she said as she turned around to apologize. "It's my fault. I—Nick!"

Nick Newton was Glacier Fall's newest resident, who also happened to be extremely handsome and ridiculously wealthy and therefore was the most sought-after bachelor in town. Never mind the fact that he had the sweetest little baby girl and pulled off the single dad thing adorably—not that Charlotte was in the market for a new boyfriend, because she absolutely was not. But she liked Nick. He was kind and sweet and a little bit dorky. And his baby, Amelia, was just about the most gorgeous child she'd ever seen. Charlotte couldn't help it; she had a soft spot for babies.

"Charlotte." Nick's face transformed into a smile. He always looked a little tired, but was it Char's imagination, or did he look stressed out, too? "I'm so sorry," he continued. "I didn't mean to crash into you. Are you okay?"

She rubbed her arm in reflex. "I'm fine. Totally my fault. I just walked in and the honey buns smelled so good, I couldn't take another step forward."

He laughed. "It *does* smell good in here. And that's exactly why we're here. A honey bun and some much needed coffee. Will you join us?"

It wasn't the only reason Nick was in the bakery that morning. Although, more often than not, Sweetie Pies was becoming his go-to breakfast place. He really was going to have to develop a few skills in the kitchen and soon, or he was going to gain twenty pounds and Amelia's first word would be sugar, for all the time he spent at the bakery.

But that morning, it was more than just the lure of sugar and caffeine that had brought him to the bakery. Nick needed to think. And oddly enough, he'd always done his best thinking when he was surrounded by people in a busy place. His friend and old business partner, Damon, had needed silence to do his work, insisting that a quiet space allowed his mind to take over and the ideas to come to him. But Nick was the opposite. The quiet made it impossible to silence his own thoughts long enough to get the answers he needed.

And he needed answers.

After Amelia's early morning wake-up, he'd been unable to get back to sleep and had instead decided to do a little more research into his situation before calling his lawyer at the much more reasonable hour of five a.m. Nick knew Chris was awake, and no doubt already at his desk. He was the only person who worked harder than Nick and Damon—when they'd been working on their design—which was why Chris Montgomery had been the perfect choice for their team.

He hadn't been surprised to hear from Nick, either. "Have you thought more about your situation?" Chris never was one for small talk.

"It's all I can think about."

Chris was one of the very few people who knew the truth about baby Amelia's parentage. At least as much as anyone knew. Only Jessica knew who her father actually was. At least, Nick assumed she knew. But that could turn out to be a pretty big assumption, given Jessica's lifestyle at the time.

"And?" Chris had presented Nick with a few options for how to proceed with Amelia. There was only one really good choice, but that didn't stop Nick from feeling badly about it. "Nick, you know there's only one thing to do."

He did know.

"If you want that little girl to stay with you, it's the only choice."

Nick swallowed. "I know."

"So you want me to proceed with adoption?"

He nodded. "Yes."

Adoption would mean that Amelia was his and no one could take her from him. He had the best legal team money could buy, and Chris had assured him that they'd do everything they could to make it come together quickly and as painlessly as possible. Which no doubt also meant it would cost him. But Nick didn't care. He only cared about making sure Amelia's future was secure and safe.

He'd grown up without a father. And a mother who might as well have not been there most of the time, she was so lost in addiction. To both men and alcohol. It wasn't fair to compare

Jessica with his mother, not when he didn't know. Not really. But it also wasn't fair to Amelia to roll those dice. She deserved more than the start he got in life, and he would go to the ends of the earth to give it to her.

Chris had spent the next fifteen minutes reminding him that it wouldn't be easy, and they'd have to contact the birth mother, get her to sign over parental rights or have her proved unfit, neither of which was what Nick wanted to hear. And he'd told him as much. If Jessica didn't agree, it could get messy and Amelia didn't deserve that. He also knew, thanks to Chris, that it wasn't easy for a single father to proceed with adoption, particularly when he wasn't actually the biological father.

Still. There weren't any other options.

Nick had agreed to send over the information from the private investigator regarding Jessica's whereabouts and put the wheels in motion.

But that was a few hours ago, and he still hadn't sent it. Because he knew exactly what would happen if he did.

Everything would change, and the peaceful, little, quiet life he'd been trying to build in Glacier Falls would become anything but.

At least for the time being, he could enjoy the quiet…and Charlotte. Nick snuck a glance back toward the table where he'd left her and Amelia to get settled while he went to grab coffee and snacks.

He smiled the way he always seemed to when he saw Charlotte Davis. From the first time he'd met her, something drew him to her. Sure, he knew she was coming out of a terrible relationship and was not in any way ready to date again, but he wasn't either. It was a detail that almost made him like her more. She was sweet and funny and absolutely stunning. Something about her—a quiet, thoughtful undercurrent—let Nick know there was a lot more to her than she showed people on the surface. In a different situation, he would have already asked her out.

Charlotte wasn't like any of the women he'd met before. Which wasn't too hard a feat, really, considering when he and Damon were busy at work on their microchip design, there hadn't been any time for women, and definitely no time for dating. When he was invested in a project, he went all in, with complete focus.

When they'd finally finished and sold the microchip design for more money than either Nick or Damon could properly understand, Nick had gone completely off the rails and, true to form, became one hundred percent invested in the party lifestyle. Women and partying. Traveling the globe. Drinking too much everywhere he went and largely living a life that had started to scare him on more than one occasion. He'd woken up more than once unsure of where he was, who he was with, or how he'd gotten there.

He might still be that way, too, if Amelia hadn't come into his life. Because the moment the baby girl was dropped in his lap, once again his focus shifted—one hundred percent. Only now he was completely devoted to a tiny baby girl.

And that's where his focus would stay, at least until she was legally his and safe from the type of childhood he'd grown up with. Maybe then…he'd be able to expand his attentions and think about finding someone to share his life with. His gaze lingered on Charlotte, who'd pulled Amelia from her stroller and bounced her on her lap, making the baby giggle. He smiled, a warmth in his chest beginning to grow. *Maybe even—*

"Hey, handsome."

He spun around to see Georgia behind the counter, her trademarked bright smile on her face.

"What can I get you? Something sweet, I hope?" She lowered her eyelids and wiggled her eyebrows.

"Sorry." Nick shook his head. "I was daydreaming for a minute."

"About me, I hope?"

"Always." He couldn't help but return the innocent flirting. "And those sweet buns of yours." Georgia was one of those women who made it easy to flirt with them. She was bubbly and fun, and every morning when he dragged his exhausted self into her bakery, she was there with a smile and a coffee. Two of his favorite things.

They exchanged a few more minutes of banter while Nick placed his standard order, adding an extra coffee and bun for Charlotte, an addition that earned him an extra eyebrow raise and a glance in Charlotte's direction. There was a question in Georgia's eye, but Nick didn't rise to the bait.

If he was ever ready to date again, Georgia should be an obvious candidate. She was easygoing, fun, flirty, and cute. She owned her own business and as far as Nick knew, she had her life together and was in a good place. On paper, she seemed like a perfect choice for dating. But something was missing. Something he couldn't quite pinpoint.

He accepted his order and paid, leaving a generous tip the way he always did. When she gave him a wink as a thank-you, he returned it with one of his own before taking the tray and turning around.

The moment Nick saw Charlotte and Amelia together, a giant smile crossed his face again and once more the warmth in his gut bloomed. Seeing her with Amelia stirred up all kinds of really good feelings he didn't have any real experience with, and more importantly, whatever was missing when he looked at Georgia fell perfectly into place when he looked at Charlotte.

Chapter Two

"COME ON, Jeremy. It'll be fun."

Charlotte flopped on her baby brother's couch and clutched at the bright-red throw pillow she didn't recognize. It screamed of a female touch. For sure, Jeremy's fiancée Bella Burton, who was away most of the time in LA shooting her debut breakout movie, *Bombshell*, had given it to him.

"No way." He grabbed two beers out of the fridge and turned around as Charlotte tossed the pillow at him. It bounced off his chest to the floor. "Hey. Bella gave me that."

"I figured." She laughed. "No way would you have decorative pillows in your man space."

Jeremy handed her a beer, grabbed the pillow, and sat across from her on his couch. "What can I say?" He shrugged. "She makes my life better in all the ways."

"That's the truth." Not that Jeremy wasn't an awesome guy before Bella came along into his life, but Charlotte had to admit that the almost crazy-famous woman had brought a new spark into her brother's world. He'd just officially become Glacier Falls' new fire chief and now, newly engaged to Bella, Charlotte's little brother seemed to finally have it all together.

Now it was her turn.

"Just think," she said. "With me living here, I could bring even more female influences into your life. It would be—"

"No."

"Jer! Come on. I can't stay at Mom and Dad's. They're…"

She didn't know how to finish that sentence. Not really. They were awesome. The best parents she could ask for, that much was very true. They'd been nothing but supportive of everything she'd ever done. When she wanted to go to interior design school instead of business college, they hadn't blinked. When she decided to sell everything and move to the other side of the country, they were encouraging. And most importantly, when Jeremy had arranged with a fire chief in Halifax to get her safely home back to Glacier Falls and away from Billy before his control became more extreme because she was terrified of him, they'd accepted her back into her childhood home with open arms and no questions asked. Even though she knew her mother was dying to know what had happened and how her strong, capable, confident daughter could have succumbed to such a man.

"They're great," she finished lamely.

"But they're Mom and Dad," Jeremy said. "I get it."

She took a sip of her beer and made a face. It had been awhile since she'd had a beer. It wasn't bad, just different. She tried again, and Jeremy laughed.

"I understand *why* you want to move in here," he said. "But you know you can't."

"You're here alone most of the time," Charlotte protested. "And that's if you're not in LA with Bella while she's shooting. I could take care of your place, make sure it's lived in."

He laughed and shook his head. "I have no doubt you'd take very good care of my place, but it's not going to be long before Bella's done shooting and then she'll be back here a lot more."

Charlotte didn't bother bringing up the fact that Bella would still be gone a lot. With publicity tours, new roles, a recording deal, and more and more opportunities that were popping up for her all the time, there was no doubt that Bella would be very busy and away from Glacier Falls for long periods of time. But Jeremy knew that. He didn't need his older sister bringing it up again. Besides, Char had to admit, the couple was handling the distance really well. If anyone could manage the balance, it would be Jeremy and Bella. She also knew that asking Jeremy to move in to his place was a total long shot, and she didn't blame him at all for saying no.

She'd expected it.

He gave her a look over his beer bottle, while he took a long pull, and she sighed, resigned.

"I know. I know. I'll figure something else out."

They sat in companionable silence for a few minutes. It had always been easy to just *be* with Jeremy. Charlotte had missed it, and she didn't even really notice how much until she had it back.

"Is living with Mom and Dad so bad?" Her brother put his beer bottle down and crossed his leg over his knee as he leaned back into the couch.

"You know it's not." She smiled, but couldn't keep it up. "It's just...I'm thirty-two, Jer. I want...no, I *need* to move on and show them their baby girl isn't broken. I don't need to be handled with kid gloves. Do you know Mom is making me breakfast every day?"

Jeremy shook his head and chuckled. "I didn't know that."

Charlotte leaned forward. "Two eggs, scrambled, with toast and grapefruit slices."

He raised his eyebrows.

"And she peels the grapefruit."

"That sounds pretty good, if you ask me." He laughed

again and Char had to fight the urge to throw a pillow at him. "But you don't like it?"

She rolled her eyes. "Jer, I haven't eaten breakfast in at least five years. But if I tell Mom that, she'll get all worried and go on about how much weight I've lost."

"She's not wrong."

"I'm fine." Charlotte crossed her arms over her chest like a child. A moment later, she smiled. "Honestly, I am fine. I've been seeing my therapist, and she's really helped me understand why I made the choices I did. I think I just need a little space to really…you know."

"Grow up?"

She did throw the pillow at him then.

"What I really need is a job. A real job," she amended. "I know Mom and Dad only hired me because they felt bad for me. It's part-time and doesn't pay anything. And please don't tell them, but I hate it. It's torture looking at such terrible real estate photos. I mean, do people really have no concept of interior design?"

"Not everyone *is* an interior designer, Char." He gave her a pointed look. "Why don't you offer your services? That is what you do, right?"

It was what she did. Before she'd dropped everything to move cross country, Charlotte had a great job with a new home builder in the city. She did all the staging for the show homes and picked out paint colors, tile, and carpet choices. She'd loved it. It had been the first time she'd really felt productive and good at her job. But even if she was to get that job back, she'd have to move to the city and both she and her therapist, Lauren Hayes, had agreed that she should stay in Glacier Falls for both safety and protection. Not that she thought Billy would come after her. Not really. After a few threatening calls, he'd petered out, just the way she'd hoped he would.

Billy would have made it really hard for her to leave, but he was a weak man, and she was sure that once he realized she'd left, he'd let it go. His pride wouldn't let him go after her. He'd never want to be in a position of being seen as *begging*. Charlotte was confident he wouldn't go to any great lengths to get her back. He just wasn't that driven of a person.

"It's what I *did*," Char corrected her brother. "I mean, I'd love to do it again one day, but what are the odds of that happening in Glacier Falls?"

In her pocket, her cell phone vibrated with an incoming call. Only a handful of people had her new number, and of those few, it was usually her mother or father calling to check on her, so she almost ignored it. But curiosity got the best of her, especially when an unknown number was displayed on the screen.

Jeremy shrugged. "Answer it."

So she did. "Hello?"

"Charlotte Davis?" The female voice didn't sound threatening in any way. In fact, it sounded a little familiar, so Char answered. "Oh good," the woman continued. "This is Stephanie Starz. We met at the—"

"I remember." How could you *not* remember Stephanie Starz? She was quite literally the biggest movie star in the world, who also happened to be a very good friend of her brother's fiancée, Bella, and was the newest resident of Glacier Falls, even if currently she was spending most of her time away filming or in the city three hours away dealing with the various other aspects of fame.

"Oh good," Stephanie continued. "I wasn't sure you would. Listen, I won't keep you, and I hope you don't mind, but I got your number from Nick Newton. He's a good friend of mine."

Char's face flushed at the mention of Nick's name. She

didn't know him well yet, but he was her newest friend. And every time she saw him, she couldn't help but feel drawn to the single dad. He was sweet and funny and…he was nice to be around.

"Right," she said lamely, both flustered by the mention of Nick *and* the call from a mega celebrity. Jeremy raised an eyebrow in question, but she looked away. "How can I help you?"

Stephanie jumped right into it. "I don't know if you've heard, but I'm developing the old fishing camp cabins at Lynx Creek."

Of course she'd heard. Everyone had heard. It was huge news. She nodded despite the fact that Stephanie couldn't see her. Not that it mattered, because the other woman was still talking.

"Anyway," she said. "I want to hire you to do the interior work on them. I'm just too busy with everything and I'm told you're really talented. So—"

"I'm sorry."

"You can't?"

"No," Char said quickly. "I'm just…what did you say? You want to hire me?" She turned to look at her brother.

Jeremy's eyes got much bigger and his mouth fell open with a shrug.

"I do. Are you available?"

"I am."

"Perfect! I have to run right now, but I'll call you soon so we can set up a meeting and talk details, okay?"

The call ended. Still in shock, Charlotte stared at the phone in wonder before looking to her brother. "Did that just happen?"

He laughed. "Looks like you might have enough money to move out after all, sis."

With the monitor in hand, Nick quietly slid the glass door to the patio closed and stepped out into the spring air to look out over the ridge. The view was amazing at ElkView Ridge, Damon and Katie Banks's property that overlooked town. Damon had graciously offered Nick and Amelia the guest house to stay in while the new place in town Nick had purchased was renovated. It was small, but it worked. And really, they didn't need much room. Even if it made nap time a little difficult.

Nick had set up a temporary *nap-time* office on the porch, complete with his laptop, a notebook, and his phone. Amelia was pretty good with her naps, but he didn't want to risk waking her up when he was on the phone, especially if he got heated and raised his voice. And he was sure to do both of those things when he talked to his lawyers lately. The last thing he wanted was to expose Amelia to that kind of negativity, even if she didn't understand it.

He put the baby monitor down next to his laptop. But before calling Chris, Nick took a moment to take in the beautiful view. He breathed deep, filling his lungs with the fresh air and exhaling slowly.

"It's pretty amazing, isn't it?" Damon joined him on the edge of the patio to gaze out over the view and the town below. "Sorry to interrupt," he said when Nick looked over at him. "I was just on my way into town and saw you."

"No." Nick waved away the explanation. "It's good to see you. I was just about to call Chris, so I could definitely use the distraction."

"Ah." Damon pressed his lips together. "The lawyer. That's either good news or..."

"It's mixed-up news." He inhaled the fresh air again, hoping it would help give him clarity. "I'm adopting Amelia."

"That's great news." Damon slapped him on the back, his grin wide. "But...wait...why would you have to adopt? I don't know how all this works, but you're her father. It's just a custody issue, isn't it? Not an..." His words faded away when Nick shook his head. "No, it's not a custody issue? Or no, you're not—"

"I'm not Amelia's father." Nick finally confessed his secret to his best friend. Besides his legal team, only Stephanie Starz knew the truth. He'd been hoping to keep it that way for Amelia's sake, but it was looking less and less likely that would be a possibility.

"I don't understand."

Nick waved to the table and the chairs around it. "Sit. It's a long story."

He poured his friend a glass of the iced tea he had set out, and filled him in on what he knew, which wasn't much but included his brief relationship with Jessica, Amelia's mother, and how she'd told her sister that he was the father—no doubt because she'd read about his massive financial success and was likely the best choice of the prospective fathers, real or not.

"But...why..." Damon clearly struggled to make sense of what Nick had told him. Or more likely, he didn't want to say it out loud.

"Why would I adopt her if she's not mine?"

Damon nodded. It was a fair question, to be sure, and one he expected to hear more than once. After all, why would a single, successful man want to willingly tie himself down with a baby who wasn't his?

As complicated as the question was, the answer was simple.

"I fell in love with her."

Damon ingested that information. He took a sip of iced tea, swallowed and nodded. "Okay."

Nick tipped his head toward his friend. "Yeah?"

"Yeah. Of course," Damon said. "You love her. You're going to fight for her."

"I am."

Damon knew about Nick's family life and his upbringing, a detail Nick was now thankful for because he didn't have to revisit it as part of the reasoning as to why he couldn't ever let Amelia experience what he had growing up. Damon understood.

"Anything you need, man. We've got your back." Damon stood and put his hand on Nick's shoulder. "Anything. Okay?"

"I appreciate it more than you know." Nick took his glasses off and rubbed the bridge of his nose before putting them back. "I'm afraid things might get complicated, and I'm not really sure what's going to happen. To legally adopt her, I need Jessica to sign over parental rights. Which is bullshit, because if you abandon your child, that should be enough."

Damon nodded sympathetically.

"Turns out it's not. Anyway, my investigators found her. I gave the legal team the info two days ago. They were presenting her with the papers today."

"Today?"

"This morning." Nick dropped his head. It had all happened so fast after he gave Chris the information of Jessica's whereabouts. But that's how it should happen, Chris told him. The faster the better. "Which is why I'm—"

"Looking like you could use a stiff drink?"

Nick burst out in a laugh. "I wish. But it's probably a little too early in the day for that. Besides, I need to be sharp when I call Chris. I have a feeling that it's not going to be as smooth as I'd like."

"But she gave up her baby. Why wouldn't it be smooth?" Damon shook his head. "Isn't this what she wanted? For you to adopt the baby? Why else would she have given her to you?"

It was exactly what Nick had been saying and thinking. But

he knew in his gut that it wouldn't be that simple. There was a reason Jessica had been working on turning her life around. She wanted her baby back.

And as much as Nick wanted to be supportive of that, his heart broke at the very thought of saying good-bye to his baby girl.

Chapter Three

THE PHONE CALL from Stephanie Starz was exactly what Charlotte needed to get her excited about things again. It hadn't even occurred to her to try to start up her own interior design business or consultation at all. She'd been so wrapped up in the mess of her personal life, she hadn't even thought such a thing was possible. But now, it felt like *anything* was possible.

She couldn't help but laugh at herself as she walked, almost ran down Main Street toward the hardware store. One phone call and her entire thought process had shifted. No doubt her therapist would have a field day with that, probably tell her how she needed to find happiness within herself before she looked outward.

And Lauren wouldn't be wrong. But a job offer from Stephanie Starz was also an equally powerful way to find some joy. And she'd take it.

She was greeted by the tinkling of bells as she pushed open the door to the hardware shop and was instantly hit with the unique blend of wood, paint, and grease that she remembered. *How long had it been?*

When she was in high school and had first developed an interest in paint colors and designs, Charlotte had spent a lot of time in Howard's Hardware, looking at paint chips, matching colors, and convincing Harriet, the owner's wife, to give her sample cans so she could test them at home. Just setting foot into the shop again bought back all those memories, and so many more. Harriet had given her a hard time at first about her paint swatches, but Charlotte knew she secretly loved her frequent visits to the shop. So much so that it wasn't long before Harriet started showing Char giant books of wallpaper samples, stencils, and catalogs for various furniture pieces they could order in.

Those early years of poring over catalogs, order books, and experimenting with color had been so important for Charlotte and were without a doubt the reason she'd pursued design as a career choice.

How could she have forgotten?

Char made her way through the aisles of the store, to the paint counter at the back. Her face lit up the moment she stepped in front of the paint chip shelves.

Home.

It had been too long since she'd lost herself in shades of gray and white. Looking for the exact right mix of cool and warm. A neutral that paired perfectly with a statement color. Char's fingers drifted toward the greens. Healing aloe, evergreens, palace green, salamander. She couldn't help but giggle at that one as her fingers pulled the card from the slot.

"Charlotte? Charlotte Davis?"

She turned to see Harriet Howard, looking just the way she'd remembered her as a young girl, if not about fifteen years older. *Had it really been that long?*

"Mrs. Howard?"

"Well, I thought that it must be you." The older woman wiped her hands on her apron and grinned. "I've only ever known one girl in all my life who smiled at paint chips like that."

Charlotte laughed and shrugged. "What can I say? There's something about all the possibilities that's exciting."

Harriet took a slow step forward. "How about a hug?"

There was no way she could turn it down. Charlotte wrapped her arms around the tiny, old woman but didn't hug too hard. Despite Harriet's own tight squeeze, the woman was so frail-looking, Char didn't want to break her. "I didn't think you'd still be here," she said when she released Harriet from the embrace. "After all these years, you're still running this store." She shook her head in wonder, but Harriet only laughed.

"Where else would I be? Besides, someone needs to keep this town supplied. Do you know we've been busier than ever with all the new construction in town? I can hardly keep up." Her voice dipped. "And when Charlie died, well, I just didn't think I could manage it myself."

Char felt an instant shot of guilt. She didn't know Harriet had lost her husband. Then again, how would she know? She hadn't really kept up with much in Glacier Falls beyond her own family. "I'm so sorry to hear that, Harriet. I had no idea."

"Time passes." Harriet shrugged. "Do you remember Brett Bryant? I think you two were about the same age in school."

Char grinned. "Of course I remember Brett. He was a few years older than me, but he was—"

"Always trying to get you to go out with me?"

"Brett!"

Without hesitation, Charlotte threw her arms around her old friend. "I had no idea you were still in town."

She was starting to say that a lot, and it was starting to get more than a little embarrassing that she hadn't paid any attention to her hometown after she left.

"I was in the city for a while," he said. "I took some

construction classes and got a diploma in business manage-ment. But there's something about Glacier Falls." He shrugged, his green eyes sparkling.

He'd always been handsome, but he'd really grown into his looks since high school. Charlotte still couldn't begin to imagine thinking of him as anything besides the boy who would tease her relentlessly for hanging out in the hardware shop where he'd worked, but even she could admit he was a good-looking man. One who clearly had a heart of gold, considering the way he put his arm around Harriet and pulled her close.

"Besides, when I heard that Harriet needed help...well, it seemed like a good time to come home. Been back a few years now."

"He's been a lifesaver," Harriet said. "I never would have been able to keep the doors open without him." Her smile dropped. "It's not like my Zoe would ever set foot through the doors, and well..."

She drifted off, and judging by the look of warning that Brett shot her, it was obviously a sensitive subject. Zoe Howard was a few years older than Char in school as well, and she didn't know her well at all except that she'd been a bit of a handful for her parents back then, too.

"Anyway," Harriet's smile returned, "I see you looking at the paint chips, Charlotte. Are you working on another project?"

She didn't want to say anything yet, especially because she didn't officially have the job and was only there to pull together some ideas to show Stephanie. So all she said was, "It's been so long since I've looked, I was curious about the season's new colors."

It turned out to be the right thing to say, because Harriet came alive and immediately began pulling paint cards to show her. "You inspired me all those years ago, Charlotte. Ever since, I've been sure to bring in all the new trendy colors."

For the next thirty minutes, a sense of peace, happiness, and purpose washed over her as Charlotte and Harriet pored over the colors and Char started to piece together some ideas to present to Stephanie Starz. By the time she walked out the doors, her mind was bursting with ideas, and she couldn't wait to get home to start putting them all together.

"She what?"

Despite *knowing* in his gut that it wouldn't be easy, Nick still wasn't prepared for what his lawyer relayed to him.

"She didn't sign the papers?"

"No," Chris confirmed for the third time. "And she informed my team that she would be—"

"Seeking custody." Just saying the words out loud made Nick want to throw up. He glanced behind him at the guest house where his baby girl was still sleeping. He could take her and run. He had the resources that no one would ever find them. They could go off the—*no*.

That was crazy. A life on the run would be almost as bad as a life with an addict, unfit mother. And if Jessica was making changes, that wouldn't be the life at all.

If Jessica was making changes. It was a big *if*. And the even bigger *if* was if she could maintain those changes.

How many times had Nick's own mother said she was going to change and maybe even changed for a little bit before falling back into old habits? He'd lost count.

Maybe it wasn't fair to presume Jessica would do the same. Plenty of addicts turned their lives around. It happened all the time. But sometimes it didn't, and it was a pretty big gamble to take with his daughter's future. And *yes*, Amelia was his daughter. He couldn't think of her in any other way. Ever.

"So what do I do?" He interrupted Chris, who was going on about the law and parental rights and all kinds of other things. He needed the nitty-gritty. Details. Facts. What he could do to make sure they couldn't take Amelia away from him.

"To be clear," Chris started, "Jessica hasn't made any formal declaration for custody. And she never actually said that."

"You just said…"

"You didn't let me finish. She told the team she'd be contacting you. It could be as simple as just wanting to know how the child is doing. She could be calling to explain herself. The fact is, we don't know yet if custody is something she's interested in."

It was. How could it not be? How could she walk away from her child and not want her back?

"In the meantime," Chris continued, "we'll appeal to the courts for an adoption hearing. You will need to prove that you are the best possible choice to be Amelia's parent."

"No problem." Nick paced back to the table and picked up his pen, ready to take some notes. "I am the best choice."

"You think that." He could almost hear Chris sigh. "And I might even think that. But we need the courts to think that. And I have to be honest—a single dad with no history of a serious relationship, let alone no actual partner to help raise the baby, might be a hard sell."

"But I have—"

"Resources? Yes. You do. But you're going to need more than money."

Nick scribbled some notes but then lifted his head again. "More than money?"

"Yes, Nick." Chris didn't bother trying to hide his sigh this time. "More than money. You're going to need a partner."

"A partner?"

"For a genius, you're not picking up on this very quickly." Chris laughed. "Nick, you need a girlfriend. A wife, preferably. And you need one now. Actually, yesterday."

Charlotte's brain overflowed with ideas she could put together and present to Stephanie Starz for her new cabins. It was an amazing opportunity. No, it was *beyond* an amazing opportunity. It was *the* opportunity.

If she could impress Stephanie, she'd get the job. And not only would that kick-start a career she'd thought long dead, it could be the launch of an even grander career. Stephanie was *huge*. And that was an understatement.

The entire world hung off every single thing the woman did. If she chose Charlotte to design the interiors of her cabins...Char couldn't even process how major that could be for her.

Not only would she be able to afford her own apartment away from her parents, she would be able to afford...well...a life! Which was why she had to nail this meeting. Stephanie hadn't called it an interview, but it might as well be one. She was going to be in town in five days. And Char wanted to show her something that would make it almost impossible *not* to hire her.

Her mind was still preoccupied as she hustled down Main Street, eager to get home and start putting things together, when she heard a baby cry. She turned toward the grocery store, at the sound of the cry, and her stomach did that odd squeezey-flip thing it had started doing lately whenever she saw Nick Newton. Or maybe it was when she saw his baby, Amelia. She couldn't be sure. Either way, she changed course, drawn to the pair like a magnet.

"Let me take her," Char said when she got close enough to see that Nick was struggling trying to balance an arm full of groceries and the fussy baby. Before waiting for an answer, she took the baby, who almost immediately calmed in Charlotte's arms.

"I don't know how you do that." Nick shook his head in amazement and adjusted his load. "She likes you."

"You look like you have your arms full."

"I don't know what I was thinking." Nick smiled, but it didn't reach his eyes the way it usually did. "I just needed a few things, so I didn't bother with the stroller, but a few things turned into...well...I won't bore you with the details. Thank you," he added, almost as an afterthought. "Would you mind..." He used his head to gesture toward the parking lot.

"Not at all." Char focused on the baby and tickled her under her chin. "She's just so sweet." They started walking. "And you're doing it all on your own...that must be hard." Char didn't know Nick very well yet, but she did know he was a single father. From what she could tell, not many people in town knew the details about his situation. At least, if they did, they weren't talking about it.

"It is hard." He stopped at a sleek, black SUV and used his foot to wave under a sensor so the back hatch lifted.

Char lifted her eyebrows, impressed, but didn't bother saying anything.

"I don't say this very often." Nick tucked the bags of groceries inside. "But it isn't easy. And you know what's even harder?"

She stayed quiet, pretty sure it was a rhetorical question.

Sure enough, Nick finished his thought. "Navigating the whole legal system."

The comment jarred her. "Legal system? Are you being sued?"

"No." Nick turned around. "Sorry, I shouldn't have said

anything. It's just…well, let's just say, the legal system is definitely not designed to make things easy for a single dad trying
to secure custody."

"Oh. I…I had no idea it was so…" She swallowed hard.
"I'm sorry, Nick. I can't even imagine how difficult that must
be." It felt like the most inadequate thing to say, but Charlotte
really had no idea *what* to say. She wanted to ask him more
about it, but it didn't feel like the right time, and Nick didn't
seem like the kind of man to open up easily. She turned her
attention back on Amelia, who was trying to grab her hair.
"For what it's worth," Char said, "I think you're doing an
amazing job." She smiled at the baby. "I mean, look at how
happy she is all the time."

Nick chuckled. "You don't see her at four in the morning."
He reached out and tickled Amelia, who turned and beamed at
her daddy. "Someone likes to wake up nice and early these
days, don't they?"

Amelia giggled and it was just about the sweetest sound
Charlotte had ever heard.

"I'll take her," Nick said, his arms outstretched. "Thank
you so much for your help."

"Anytime." His hands brushed hers as she passed him the
baby, and her stomach clenched while a shock flew through
her. Nick hesitated, as if maybe he felt it, too. She looked up so
their eyes met and smiled.

The last thing Charlotte needed in her life was another
man. Not after the whole thing with Billy and the way that had
destroyed her. But maybe her therapist was right. Lauren had
tried to tell her that not all men were like Billy. That, in fact,
Billy was the exception, not the rule. Still. The idea of having
feelings for a man again was terrifying. How could she ever
trust her instincts after she'd gotten herself into such a terrible
situation?

Char held his gaze for a moment, but finally looked away.

She wasn't sure she could.

Mercifully, Nick turned and buckled the baby up in her car seat, giving her a few minutes to catch her breath and slow her racing heart, because her body clearly didn't get the memo that her brain was trying to send. *No men. Not now.* Besides, even if she were ready to date—which she certainly was not—a single father who was clearly having some custody issues was probably not the best choice for her to get her feet wet with.

Nick straightened up and faced her again as he ran a hand through his thick, dark hair. She couldn't help but notice the stubble on his chin. *The start of a beard maybe?* It was sexy. And there was no way she wasn't going to notice it. Or the way it made her stomach flip when he smiled at her.

Dammit.

"Thanks again, Char. I really appreciate it." His smile was deadly. "Oh," he added. "I forgot to ask you if Stephanie Starz reached out to you?"

She shook her blonde hair back over her shoulder. "She did and…oh my goodness. I'm totally spaced. Thank you so much for recommending me! She said you gave her my number and…I can't believe I forgot to thank you. I'm so sorry."

How had that slipped her mind? She should have thanked him the second she saw him. Normally she wasn't so slack on her manners. But something about Nick twisted her up inside. It wasn't an excuse for the total oversight, but still…

"Oh good." His eyes twinkled behind his glasses. "I'm glad she reached out. She needs all the help she can get with those cabins. It seemed like a perfect fit."

"I really appreciate it, Nick. I can't thank you enough. It's an amazing opportunity."

"I have no doubt you'll nail it." He smiled at her and for a brief moment, he didn't seem nearly as stressed and preoccupied as he had been a few minutes earlier. But then it was gone. Amelia let out a squeal of protest in the backseat and he shook his head, snapped back into the moment. "I should get going. I need to figure out...well, I have some things I need to think about."

And just like that, the stress and worry she'd seen in him earlier returned. Char had to wrap her arms around herself to keep from reaching out and hugging him. He looked like he could use one.

"Thanks again," she said. "I owe you one, Nick. Really. I know there's probably nothing I can do with this whole..." She waved her hand around. "But let me know if I can help in any way. I really wish I could do something."

"Sure." He chuckled, but there was no humor in it. "Looks like I need a wife. You want to marry me?"

She took a quick step back. "What?"

He roughed up his hair. "I'm kidding. Don't worry."

"Kidding about needing a wife? Or kidding about marrying me?"

He looked up and gave her a smile tinged with sadness. "Would it matter?"

She hesitated, unsure what to say.

Amelia shrieked again from her car seat, distracting them, and Nick turned to go. "Don't worry about it," he said. "It'll all work out. Thanks, Char. I'll see you around."

It'll all work out.

His words lingered in her head as she watched him drive away. She couldn't shake the terrible feeling that it wouldn't all work out.

It was clear by Katie and Damon's reaction when Nick showed up at their front door later that night with baby Amelia tucked into his arm that he looked every bit as terrible as he felt. Which was pretty bad.

After returning from his grocery trip, Nick had fed the baby and tried to eat something of his own, but he couldn't focus. His mind wouldn't stop running through scenarios. Running into Char had been a good distraction, but it had only been that. A distraction. He still didn't have any answers.

Katie scooped up the baby and ushered the men into the front room of the grand house where Damon kept the whisky. His friend poured him a stiff one and handed it to him in a crystal tumbler before taking the seat across from him.

Nick glanced around for Katie and the baby, but Damon stopped him. "It's okay. Katie's got her, and she's perfectly fine. Katie loves it and no doubt she'll want to revisit the whole *let's have kids* conversation after you leave."

Damon smiled, but Nick couldn't return it. Instead, he put the whisky down on the table in front of him and dropped his head into his hands.

Nick didn't make it a practice to leave Amelia with babysitters, even when they were in the same house. Sure, he let others hold Amelia and bounce her around. But care for her? No. That was his job. Despite his friend Stephanie's insistence that it would be fine to hire a nanny to help him out, even part-time, he couldn't bring himself to do it. He didn't want her to be raised by strangers. Besides, he had the luxury of not having to work at the moment. Amelia deserved to be raised by a parent. Or at least a…he couldn't think about *what* he was to her. Anyway, he knew he *would* have to hire a nanny or find some kind of constant babysitter situation going forward, but apparently he had bigger problems. He had to find a wife.

A wife.

The whole thing was ludicrous, and he couldn't make any sense of it.

"I take it the call with legal didn't go well."

In response, Nick lifted his shoulders and dropped them again with a sigh.

"Are you going to run?"

Damon's question shouldn't have surprised him, considering he himself had thought about it. But coming from his *by-the-book* friend, it was startling.

"We'll back you up, Nick. If you need to—"

"No." He cut him off before he had the chance to actually convince him it wasn't a terrible idea. "She doesn't deserve that kind of life."

Damon nodded a bit and took a sip of his drink. "Talk to me. What happened?"

Nick didn't hesitate. The sooner he got it off his chest, the better chance he had to make sense of any of it. "I need a wife."

Damon raised his eyebrows and smirked, but didn't say anything until Nick was done relaying the story completely.

"So," Nick wrapped it up, "if I'm going to convince the judge that I'm the best choice to legally adopt her, I need to be a family man. Stable and secure. And that's only *if* Jessica doesn't decide to come back into the picture." He sagged back against the couch. "So you see, it's a big friggin' mess."

"It definitely sounds like it." Damon raised his glass to his lips, but put it back down before speaking again. "But you've come to the right place."

Nick perked up. "You can find me a wife?"

His friend chuckled. "Do you forget how I got my own wife?" He tilted his head until Nick finally smiled, remembering that Damon himself had convinced his longtime best friend, Katie, to pretend to be his wife to satisfy some sort of crazy condition his father had on ElkView Ridge in order to buy his childhood home. "And see how that worked out?"

Nick couldn't help it; he laughed and roughed his hands through his hair. "That's different. You two were always in love with each other. And you had an obvious choice for a pretend wife."

"True." Damon put his drink down and stood, and stretched his arms over his head. "But still. I do have some experience in the area if you need a little help."

"I can't do what you did." Nick shook his head. He'd rejected the idea almost as soon as Chris suggested it. A fake wife? Even if he did think it was a good idea, where would he *find* a woman willing to go through with it? His mind flashed back to Charlotte standing next to his vehicle. *"Let me know if I can help in any way."* He almost laughed out loud. There was no way that was the kind of help she was offering. And even if he did think she was gorgeous and strong and talented, and would love to ask her out on a date if circumstances were completely different, there was no way he could ask her to do this. He needed another solution. A real one.

"Do what?" Katie reappeared with Amelia fast asleep in her arms. Nick stood by reflex and went to take the baby from her, but Katie quickly turned to the side and dodged him. "She's asleep, Nick. I like holding her. It makes me think…" She lifted her eyes in Damon's direction.

"See?" He shot a look at Nick and chuckled.

But Nick couldn't help but notice that he didn't say no. Instead, he looked at his wife with a look of love and adoration that, if Nick wasn't so stressed out, he might have made a quip about how completely whipped his best friend was.

As it was, all Nick could muster was a shrug and an honest answer. "Being a dad is pretty awesome, actually."

"See?" It was Katie's turn to shoot the pointed word at her husband before turning to Nick. "And you're doing an amazing job at it." Her smile quickly turned to a frown. "What's going on?" She glanced between the two men and back to Nick. "Damon told me there might be a…"

"Problem," Nick finished for her. "I need a wife."

Her eyes went wide and Damon filled her in on everything Nick had told him.

"Seems like an easy solution to me," Katie said when the explanation was over. "Who do we know in town who can stand in for a bit?"

"You're serious?" Nick finally reached for his whisky but still didn't take a sip.

"Totally," Katie said. "Why wouldn't I be?"

"Because it's insane?"

"Is it?" She tilted her head in challenge.

"You guys are different."

"Are we?"

Damon laughed before Nick could reply. "Katie might have a point, though, Nick. Maybe Steph would do it? That would be believable."

Nick chuckled, but there was no humor in it. The idea wasn't too farfetched. After all, they were close friends. But Stephanie was a huge international star. What would that look like?

"It can't hurt to ask," Katie said. "I mean, what's your other choice?"

In response, Nick took a sip of his drink and let the sharp liquor burn his tongue and back of his mouth before swallowing. He didn't have any other choices. That was the problem.

Chapter Four

"YOU BITCH!"

With a scream that hurt her own ears, Stephanie Starz hurled the glass she was holding in Bella Burton's direction. It shattered against the wall next to her but Bella didn't even flinch.

Damn. She was good.

"And...cut!" the director yelled. "That's a wrap, ladies! You nailed it."

Bella's pretty face split into a smile, and she crossed the distance to Steph. "Holy crap! I thought you were going to hit me with it that time."

Steph laughed. They'd already taken four takes of that scene. One where she didn't scream loud enough. One where the glass didn't shatter properly on the wall. One where the director didn't think Bella looked *angry enough*. And one where the glass had slipped from her fingers.

"Are you kidding? I would never hit you." Steph hugged her friend. "Besides, they had me practicing my aim earlier. And I used to play softball in school."

"You did not."

Steph laughed. "Okay, I didn't. But still."

Together, they walked toward their trailers. Steph knew Bella still had another scene to shoot before she wrapped for the day. But she could head home, just as soon as hair and makeup relieved her of her wig and the layers of caked-on makeup that made her look like the washed-up singer she was playing in the movie *Bombshell* alongside Bella, who had the lead as an up-and-coming star dethroning Stephanie's character as the queen of pop.

It had been a lot of fun to shoot the movie, and Steph had enjoyed it the way she always did when she was filming. But this movie was different because she was excited to get back home to Glacier Falls and her new project, Lynx Creek.

Four days left, and she'd be done and back home in the mountains.

Her new home.

She hadn't lived in Glacier Falls long, but it already felt more like home than any other place she'd ever lived. Especially now that she had the cabins at Lynx Creek. What had once been an old, abandoned fishing village was being transformed into beautiful log cabins tucked along the river, ready for a romantic retreat center.

Steph planned to live in one of them for now, but she was already starting to think about having her dream home built on the property as well. It was something she hoped to talk to Travis Bishop about when she got back to town.

Her entire body heated at the thought of the sexy, frustratingly aloof contractor who'd been working on her cabins. She'd never been so attracted to a man while at the same time being so frustrated and annoyed. It was an interesting combination, and she was still working out the balance.

Steph sat in the makeup chair and let her team go to work while she flipped her cell phone on.

Two missed calls from Nick.

She'd call him back in the morning; it was already late and Amelia would likely be sleeping.

A text from her mom.

Miss you. Hope to see you soon.

She couldn't help but feel a twinge of guilt at her mother's text. Steph missed her parents, too. It had been far too long since she'd gone home to the small town up North where she'd grown up, but she'd been even busier than usual lately with both the movie project and the cabins. And when she did have time off, she wanted to be in Glacier Falls with her new friends and her half-sisters she'd only recently reunited with. Never mind her brand-new baby nephew. There were so many draws to Glacier Falls, she'd tried to convince her parents to come visit her, even offered to have her private jet fly up and get them, but so far they'd been reluctant.

She couldn't help but feel that they were feeling displaced and maybe a bit jealous of the new family she'd found completely by accident and it hurt her heart to think that they might feel that way. She needed to make a stronger effort to show them that's not how she felt. No one could replace them. She loved them both fiercely, and she did want to share her new life with them, too. Surely they would come to see her new project at Lynx Creek; she just needed to make sure the cabins were ready.

"All done, Ms. Starz." Her makeup artist unfastened the cape and Steph was free to go, her face clean and fresh, and signature bright-red hair free of the wig she'd worn all day.

"Thank you, Missy." She hopped out of the chair. "Nothing feels as good as getting all that stuff off." She grinned. "See you tomorrow."

Her assistant was waiting outside her trailer to fill her in on the details for the next day. When Terri was finished running through the schedule, she added, "Oh. I got a call from Nick Newton."

Steph perked up.

"He insisted you call him immediately when you were free."

"He texted," Steph told her. "I'll give him a call in the morning."

Terri shook her head. "He insisted you call right away," she repeated. "Regardless of the time. He said something about it being urgent."

"Urgent? Or an emergency?"

"Urgent," she confirmed. "But between you and me, he sounded pretty panicked."

"Thank you."

Maybe it was Amelia? But if something was wrong with the baby, he would have said that. Still, it wasn't like Nick to be over-dramatic. Steph dialed his number as she got into the back of her waiting town car for the ride to her rented home.

Nick answered before the first ring was finished. "Finally. I need your help."

They'd been on the phone for over an hour and Steph was still trying to process all the things Nick was telling her.

Adoption.

A wife.

Birth mother.

A wife.

"Please don't say no."

Steph closed her eyes and leaned her head back on the couch. "You know I have to, Nick." From the moment he'd asked her, she'd known what her answer had to be. She couldn't marry Nick, or fake marry him, or even have a relationship with him. Real or otherwise. It wouldn't work. But it pained her to actually say it out loud.

"I was really hoping you wouldn't say that." Nick groaned. "But I knew you would."

"Nick, you know I would help you in a heartbeat." She sat up and rolled her shoulders. "It would be a giant PR mess and you know it. The press would have a field day with it all. It literally would be the news story of the year, and that would only hurt Amelia."

She knew Nick had to see the truth in that. The paparazzi went crazy over any story that Stephanie was involved in. And something as juicy as a marriage to a self-made billionaire that came out of nowhere would be like chum in a shark tank. Within days, they'd have the whole story figured out and they'd be exposed. It probably wouldn't damage Stephanie's career, but it would damage Nick's bid at adoption. One hundred percent. It wasn't a risk they could take, and sure enough, Nick agreed the way she knew he would.

"I knew it was a long shot," he said after a moment. "And you're right. You're just too famous, which is really too bad, because you're the best actress I know and if anyone could pretend to be madly in love with me, it would be you."

She laughed a little. "Don't sell yourself short, buddy. The right woman isn't going to have to pretend anything. You're an amazing catch and you know it."

Nick's sigh was deep and long. "The problem is, I don't have time to wait for the right woman. I need to find her now. Well, yesterday, according to my lawyer."

She felt for him, she really did. No one was more devoted to that baby than Nick. He deserved to be her father. No matter what. But Steph also knew that a judge wouldn't see it quite that simply. "I think your best bet will be to ask someone who likes you. Someone you know already. And someone who's good with—I know!" The idea hit her so hard and fast she jumped up out of the chair. "Jeremy Davis's sister! She was at the showcase and then I saw you with her at my nephew's welcoming party last time I was in town. Charlotte!"

Why hadn't she thought of it before? It was perfect. Every time she'd seen Nick and Charlotte Davis together, there seemed to be a little something between them. A flirtation. An interest. Maybe they didn't even realize it yet, but it was obvious that they liked each other. "Yes," Steph continued. "She's cute and you obviously like her and—"

"No."

"No?" Confused, she shook her head. "No, you don't like her?"

"No. I *do* like her. I actually, really like her. If things were different and I didn't have…well, things aren't different. But no, I can't ask her."

"That's stupid. She's the perfect choice."

"I can't, Steph. Remember why she's back in town?"

"Oh."

"Right."

"Right," Steph agreed. She'd forgotten about that little detail. "How's she doing?"

"Not good enough for me to ask her to marry me." He groaned and Steph couldn't help but smile a little. "I mean, I think that's a pretty big jump, don't you?"

She had to agree. "I'm sorry, Nick. But you'll think of something."

He didn't sound as though he agreed, but after they chatted for a few more minutes, at least he didn't sound quite so defeated. She was confident that although the answers weren't presenting themselves to Nick right now, they would. He was a resourceful guy.

"And I'll be in town in a few days," she said before they hung up. "I promise I'll help you out as much as I can, okay? It'll be okay, Nick. I promise."

Too bad it was a promise Stephanie had no idea whether she'd be able to keep.

Chapter Five

THINGS WERE MOVING QUICKLY. Almost too quickly. Nick barely had a chance to keep things straight in his head. After discussing it at length with his legal team and getting a little bit more advice from Damon and Katie, Nick's first response had been to hire someone to be his girlfriend or fiancée. Or whatever made sense. And that was the entire problem. None of it made sense.

He couldn't hire someone. It was ludicrous. And the idea was dismissed.

The only option would have been if he had a female friend who was willing to turn their life upside down for him and Amelia. But he didn't. It was way too big of an ask for Stephanie, and she was right. She was way too famous for it to work with her.

There were no other options. He'd made his decision, and Chris had filed the paperwork with his current—and truthful—situation. He was single. And now he'd have to face the caseworker.

He'd been hoping to put it off a little longer, but it seemed that the universe had a funny way of working. Because as soon as Chris processed the application for adoption, it had immediately triggered the system, and a caseworker had already been in touch for a preliminary meeting.

Apparently it didn't usually happen so quickly, but there was something about an opening and the woman passing through town and it all worked out. Nick didn't question it because as far as he was concerned, the faster they could get everything done with, the better. Or in this case, as soon as they could get started with what would surely be a huge fight and ongoing legal battle for him to convince the courts that even though he was a single man with a history of partying and womanizing, with no biological relation to the child, he was absolutely the best candidate.

Even he had trouble buying it.

He'd been hoping to get to Sweetie Pies early for his meeting to find a good table, get Amelia set up in a high chair and most importantly, get himself a strong coffee, but as was way too familiar these days, he was running behind. He'd made the rookie mistake of dressing Amelia before feeding her and of course, the baby chose today to smash yams all through her hair and pretty dress that Katie had brought over for the occasion. After a quick bath and a change of clothes, he'd be lucky at this point to have enough time to order before Susan Johnson arrived.

Mercifully, the bakery was surprisingly not busy when he got there. And after a quick scan of the room, it looked as if he'd beat Susan there as well. Nick wheeled the stroller to a table by the window, and leaving Amelia where he could see her, he went to the counter to give his order.

As always, Georgia's smile was warm and flirty as she took his order, and the ridiculous thought flashed through his brain that maybe he could ask her to fill in as his fiancée. But he dismissed the idea almost immediately. He barely knew her. Although she seemed like a genuinely nice woman, she could have some sort of sinister past that he had no idea about and would only make everything a million times worse. It wasn't likely, and Nick felt bad for thinking something so terrible about the woman who handed him his coffee, but he was not in a good state of mind.

She finished preparing his order and when he held out his cash, she waved it away. "It's on me."

He tilted his head in question and she grinned.

"In fact," Georgia said. "I was thinking maybe we could go out sometime."

Oh shit.

He couldn't even begin to process what dating Georgia would mean right now. Hell, what dating *anyone* would mean. *He had one focus and—* The subject of his focus, Amelia, let out a shriek of delight behind him. Coffee forgotten, he spun on his heel to see his baby girl laughing and hitting her stuffed toy against the bar of her stroller in pure glee. He followed her gaze to see what was making Amelia so happy and reflexively, he, too, smiled.

Charlotte.

⎯⎯⎯

She couldn't help it. The moment Charlotte saw the baby in her stroller, it was like a gravitational pull. Amelia smiled and when Charlotte stuck out her tongue, she giggled, and then... Charlotte couldn't be stopped. Her need for caffeine forgotten, she moved closer to the stroller and started making faces at Amelia.

Every time Amelia laughed, Charlotte laughed, which caused the baby to laugh even louder. When finally Amelia let out a shriek in the small bakery, Char glanced up toward Nick at the counter.

Her eyes met his, and she shrugged, using a series of

gestures to ask whether she could pick the baby up. Nick nodded with a grin, and it was the only invitation Charlotte needed.

"Aren't you just the cutest little girl in the whole world?" she murmured as she unclipped Amelia and lifted her into her arms. The baby giggled and Char lifted her up so she could blow a raspberry on her belly, making her laugh even harder. "You are the sweetest thing in the whole wide world, aren't you?"

Char could lose herself all day in the sweet sounds of a baby laughing. There was something so profoundly pure and innocent, as if nothing else mattered. It was quickly becoming her favorite thing to do. The idea boards, paint and fabric samples she'd tucked into her bag to show Stephanie Starz were all temporarily forgotten as she lost herself in the baby.

"Excuse me."

The voice behind her jarred Charlotte from her focus on Amelia. She pulled the baby close to her chest and turned to see a large woman with an even larger bag draped over her arm, standing directly behind her.

"My name is Susan Johnson. I'm the caseworker," the woman said, as if that were supposed to explain everything. "This must be Amelia." She reached out and tried to tickle the baby's chin, but Amelia immediately shied away and tucked her face into Charlotte's chest.

Char glanced to the counter where Nick was watching, almost frozen in place with wide eyes, and all at once, everything fell into place.

The legal system is definitely not designed to make things easy for a single dad trying to secure custody.

She looked back to Susan, and then the baby cuddled tightly in her arms. She owed Nick a favor. A *big* one. And hadn't he just told her without really telling her that he needed help?

"Yes. This is Amelia." Char shifted the baby and extended her hand. "And I'm Charlotte."

"Charlotte?" Susan shook her hand. "And who are you to baby Amelia? Are you a friend of Nick Newton's?"

A friend? Yes. She was definitely a friend. A friend who owed him a favor.

Looks like I need a wife. You want to marry me?

She didn't even know what she was agreeing to, or what she was doing. All she knew was that there was a little girl whose well-being depended on a lot of things going right. "I guess you could say that," she heard herself saying as Nick joined them, coffees in hand. She put the biggest, brightest smile on her face that she could. "I'm Nick's fiancée. I'm so glad you could make it out to meet with us."

Fiancée?

Nick almost choked. *Had she...what had she...*

He glanced from Charlotte to Susan back to Charlotte.

He put the coffees down on the table to keep from dropping them—which, by the way his hands shook, was going to be a very real possibility—and extended his hand to the caseworker. "Hello," he said as smoothly as possible. "You must be Susan. Thank you for coming out so quickly. And I didn't realize you'd have a chance to meet..." He glanced to Charlotte.

"Your fiancée?" Susan finished for him and gave him a strange look.

"Right." He recovered quickly. "Sorry, it's still all so new, and you know..."

"I didn't know you were engaged to be married." Susan watched him with one eye while she pulled out a folder and scribbled something down. "I would have expected that would be in the file here. It's an important detail." She looked up at first Nick and then Charlotte, who was the first to recover.

"Like Nick said, it really is all still so new. We decided to just go for it and we're so thrilled, but we haven't been able to find a minute to even get a ring."

A ring?

Shit.

Nick glanced to Charlotte's unadorned left hand. He hadn't thought of that. But to be fair, he hadn't thought Charlotte was going to jump in to be his *fiancée*. No, when he'd woken up, that was definitely not part of the plan. But…wow. If he could get his brain to catch up to what was happening, he might be able to start thinking logically and understand the ramifications of what she'd just done. But right now, he was in total survival mode. "Sorry," he said to both women, no longer really sure what exactly he was apologizing for. "It's just been so…well, you know how it is with a baby. The sleep deprivation will be the death of us all."

He smiled at Amelia, who waved her arms in his direction. His heart instantly swelled and he remembered exactly why he was putting himself through all this. It was for her. All of it. The lies and stories would be worth it if it meant she got to stay with him permanently.

"Oh, I remember those days myself." Susan smiled kindly as she sat heavily in the chair. "If she's keeping you up at night all of a sudden, she might be working on a tooth." She directed the comment toward Charlotte, who didn't miss a beat.

"You know, I think she might be." Charlotte smiled at Amelia, who immediately giggled.

Nick stood, transfixed, and more than a little stunned at how things were playing out. But he needed to get hold of the situation. And soon. He needed to— "Susan, do you want to hold her?"

He surprised himself with the question, but the woman

seemed delighted by the offer. "I...well...yes," she finally settled. "I think that's probably a good idea."

"Great." Nick nodded at Charlotte, who handed the baby to Susan. "Char, can I get your help for a second? I want to grab some cream and sugar." He raised his eyebrows and thankfully Char followed him quickly without question.

As soon as they were far enough away, Nick whispered, "What are you doing?"

"I told you I'd help you however I could." She kept a smile on her face, but Nick didn't miss the flash of doubt in her eyes. "You mentioned how hard it is for a single dad to get custody. The opportunity presented itself, so I'm helping."

"I didn't..." He stopped himself at the look of intense concern written all over her face. She had no way of knowing that he already had things figured out. Her motives were good. She really was trying to help. Besides, it wasn't the time to go into the details of it all. "Okay. But you know you're committed now."

She hesitated but nodded. "Anything you need, we got this."

Together, they gathered up a little jug of cream and a selection of sugars before they turned to head back to the table. Char stopped him before they moved. "I'm supposed to meet Stephanie Starz here for a meeting. Should I call her and—"

"No." He shook his head quickly. "This shouldn't take too long." He sure hoped it wouldn't, because if Susan asked any questions that they didn't have answers for—which would be all of them—they were going to be in big trouble. "Follow my lead here, okay? If she asks any questions about...well, anything."

"Got it." Char nodded. "I know I probably should have thought it out first...but I'm here to help, Nick. I'm sorry if I—"

"Don't worry about that right now, okay?" He reached out

and lifted her chin gently so she was looking at him. It was a tender touch and if it had been under any other circumstances, he might have followed it up with...*no*. He couldn't even let himself think of Charlotte in any other way. Especially now.

Nick waited until Char's eyes cleared. She nodded and offered him a small smile. "Great," he said, releasing her and immediately missing the feel of her skin under his touch. "Let's go dazzle."

They probably didn't dazzle, but to Nick's pleasant surprise, they did make Susan laugh a few times. Nick did his best to keep the conversation light and focused primarily on Amelia.

"Okay," Susan finally said as she set her now-empty coffee cup down and reached for her notebook. "Let's talk next steps."

"Next steps?" Nick nodded knowingly despite the fact that he didn't know anything. "What does that look like?"

"Well, it's my understanding that you've requested an expedited process." She looked up to meet his eyes. He nodded sharply and she refocused on the notebook, scribbling something down on the pages. "So, the next thing is we'll have a home visit, where I can assess you all in your home together and—"

"That could be difficult," Nick interrupted. Realizing how it sounded, he amended quickly, "It's just that I'm temporarily living in the guest suite of a friend's place. I'm having—we're having—" He shot a smile at Charlotte, who'd grabbed his hand under the table. If he hadn't been so distracted by the panic coursing through him at the idea of Susan visiting *their* home when it wasn't actually *theirs* at all, he might have been able to appropriately respond to the feel of her skin on his. As it was, it was probably a good thing that he was distracted because having any actual feelings for Charlotte was definitely not part of what was turning out to be a whole lot more complicated of a plan than he'd originally thought. "We're having a house in town renovated," Nick continued. "Our guest suite is pretty tight and we're—"

"That's fine." Susan grinned. "I've made a note that it's only temporary. I'm sure that with your financial means, your permanent residence will be more than adequate as well. But that's not what this visit is all about."

"It's not?"

"No." Susan spoke while she scribbled notes that Nick desperately wanted to see in her notebook. "It's more about getting a feel for the family and their dynamic. Just to assess the vibe of the family and the general fit."

The vibe?

Nick just swallowed and nodded. "Of course. Makes sense."

He squeezed Charlotte's hand under the table, which had the unexpected effect of calming him. That had never happened with a woman before. Even if it was completely unplanned, it was nice to know that she was there for him and no doubt would help him do whatever it took. Including a home visit. "Why don't we schedule that for next week some-time?" Nick suggested as he looked over to Charlotte. "Does that work for—"

"Oh no," Susan interrupted. "We don't schedule these visits."

"What?" It was Charlotte who asked. "What does that mean?"

The older woman smiled as if she enjoyed keeping people on their toes, which she probably did. It was part of her job, after all. "The idea is to make sure you're natural and not overly prepared, so we can get a real idea of what things are like in your home. So, we'll give you a window of..." She scratched a few more things down. "No later than three to five weeks."

"Three to five weeks?" Nick couldn't help the outburst. "I thought you were expediting things?"

"I assure you, Mr. Newton. That *is* expedited. And you never know, I could pop in anytime."

Nick was about to complain, but fortunately for him, Stephanie chose that moment to walk into the bakery for her meeting with Charlotte.

"Normally in situations like these—is that…"

Nick knew without turning around who had just walked in and he couldn't help but smile.

"*Stephanie Starz?*"

"It is," Nick said as Stephanie spotted them and raised her eyebrows in question. No doubt wondering why Charlotte was sitting next to him when he'd decided that there were no options but the truth.

Still, the professional she was, Stephanie's face instantly smoothed into an easy smile. She offered them a little wave and made her way to the counter to place her order.

"You know her?" Susan was completely star-struck. "Do you think maybe I could meet her?"

"Normally, I'd say yes," Nick said with a glance to Charlotte, "but she's actually here to meet with Charlotte about a business opportunity and—" He didn't bother saying how Glacier Falls was Steph's safe place, where hardly anyone bothered her with her celebrity status and he wanted to respect that for her and not exploit his famous friend, but Susan got the point.

"Oh, of course." Susan tried and failed to hide her disappointment. "Maybe some other time?"

"You know what?" Char gave his hand one final squeeze and stood. "The meeting can wait a few minutes, I'm sure. I'll go ask her if she can spare a few minutes."

Nick jumped to his feet, his hand still in Charlotte's. "You don't have to—"

"Don't worry."

She turned to him so casually and with such a sweet, natural smile as she reached over and touched his cheek gently, that, in a heartbeat, everything with Charlotte felt one thousand percent real. But when she leaned forward and gave him a soft kiss on his lips, he was completely hooked. It was the quickest of kisses, only lasting a fraction of a second, but it might as well have lasted hours for the feelings and sensations that passed between them in that instant. Nick knew she felt it, too, because when she pulled back, she looked a little stunned before blinking hard.

And then, once more her sweet smile was in place. "I'm sure she won't mind," she finished. "I'll be right back."

Nick watched Charlotte approach Steph and have a quick conversation as next to him, Susan prattled on about how she was Stephanie Starz's biggest fan and had seen all her movies, as if she hadn't even seen what had just transpired between Nick and Charlotte, which likely was exactly the case. After all, they were supposed to be a couple. An innocent kiss was expected. But not for him. And even when Steph turned in their direction with her trademarked dazzling smile, it took all the focus he could muster to return the smile and lift his hand in a wave before both Steph and Charlotte joined them.

Having Stephanie show up right when she did turned out to be exactly what Charlotte needed. With the caseworker completely star-struck and distracted, Char could make her exit and take a few minutes to catch her breath. Although she was going to need a whole lot more than a few minutes to catch her breath. She'd said her good-byes and retreated to the bathroom to compose herself.

The moment the door shut, she leaned back against the door and took a breath.

What had she just done?

Char ran the water in the tap and stared at her reflection in the mirror. Had she really just told a stranger—a caseworker—that she was Nick Newton's fiancée? Had she really just put his entire custody fight at risk because she thought she was doing him a *favor*?

She blinked hard.

He'd gone along with it, but he'd been surprised. *Very* surprised. Had she screwed things up?

And what did it mean now that she'd publicly declared they were engaged?

So many questions. And no doubt, there would be some kind of major debrief. There had to be. But she still had the meeting with Stephanie Starz to get through. The meeting that Nick had helped arrange. The whole reason she'd felt as though she owed him in the first place.

But the kiss. The *kiss?* She'd kissed him because not only did it seem like the right thing to do in that moment, but she'd *wanted* to. If she was honest, ever since she'd met him, she'd wanted to kiss him. Even though she'd met him almost immediately after returning home to Glacier Falls in the worst of situations, she'd always felt a draw to Nick. And…then with this situation, it just felt right. After all, they were trying to convince this woman they were a couple, right?

She could justify the kiss any way she wanted, but it wasn't the actual kiss that was the issue; she knew that. It was the way he'd looked at her after. It was in that moment she knew that he'd felt it, too. They might be entering into the biggest game of pretend she'd ever played, but underneath it, there was definitely something real. She just had no idea what that was, or what she was ever going to do about it.

Char shook her head in an effort to clear her thoughts.

It didn't work. There was no way she'd be able to think straight for this meeting.

Char bent down and splashed the ice-cold water on her face before turning the taps off and pulling a paper towel out to pat her face dry. The cold water helped. She took a deep breath, inhaling through her nose and exhaling hard from her mouth the way her therapist had coached her.

Inhale calm.

Exhale stress.

Repeat.

After a few moments, she wasn't feeling calm exactly, but she was no longer feeling as if she might jump out of her own skin. An improvement, to be sure.

Charlotte readjusted her tote bag on her shoulder, took one last deep breath, and headed back out to the coffee shop.

Stephanie was just finishing up with Susan, and was signing her notebook. The same notebook she'd been scribbling notes about their meeting in. She could only hope that was a good sign. As she rejoined the small group, Nick reached out and, as if it were the most natural thing in the world, wrapped his arm around her waist and pulled her close to him. He bent and whispered into her ear, "We're going to have a lot to talk about, aren't we?"

It was a huge understatement. Charlotte couldn't help but giggle as she nodded.

Amelia was asleep in her stroller now, a thumb in her mouth. So innocent. So peaceful. With no idea that her whole world could potentially be turned upside down.

Not if I can help it.

The thought filled her with unexpected passion. Char still wasn't even one hundred percent sure what her role would be, or what exactly she was going to be able to do about anything, but whatever she *could* do, she would. Of that much she was sure.

The conversation around her was wrapping up, and Char forced herself to refocus.

"It was really nice meeting you," Steph said to Susan with a practiced smile. "But I really do need to steal Charlotte here for a quick meeting. Maybe we'll see you again?"

"Oh! I…well…I mean…maybe…" Susan's face blazed red, but it was easy to see that she would love nothing more than to see Stephanie Starz again. In an effort to regain her professionalism, she turned to Charlotte. "I will definitely be seeing you again."

"Yes." Char nodded. "I look forward to it."

"Enjoy your meeting," Nick said. "I'll see you at home."

Home.

Char nodded as Nick pressed a kiss to her temple. Such a small, simple action. One that couples everywhere did without even thinking. But they *weren't* a couple, and the kiss fired through her entire body in a sizzle.

Somehow, she managed to keep it together long enough to follow Steph across the small bakery to a table in the back corner where they could have a little bit of privacy. Up until an hour ago, it was *this* meeting she'd been all worked up for, and now…she could barely process the feelings and emotions slamming into her at a shockingly intense rate.

"You good?" Steph smiled and sat across from her. "Do you need a coffee?"

"Maybe something stronger?"

Stephanie laughed and the sound dissolved some of the lingering tension.

"It might be a little early for that," Steph said. "But I wouldn't blame you for needing a stiff drink. I assume that you…well, I know Nick's situation, and if you just volunteered for what I think you did…damn. I'm impressed."

Char shook her head, still not entirely sure what, in fact, she had just volunteered for. "I don't know if you should be impressed," she said honestly. "I really hope I didn't screw things up for him and…well…you know…maybe we should talk about your cabins."

The shift in topic was exactly the distraction Charlotte needed. She pulled out her portfolio with the stack of ideas she'd been working on for Steph to check through. For the next hour, the two women pored over Char's idea books, sketched out some new thoughts about the direction Steph was hoping to go with, and completely immersed themselves in all things design to the point that Char was able to forget, even if only for a few minutes, about the mess she'd just gotten herself tangled up in.

Chapter Six

AFTER FINALLY SEEING Susan Johnson into her car outside of Sweetie Pies, Nick stood and waited until he saw her car turn left to head out of town and back to the city. Still, he waited another few minutes to make absolutely sure she was gone before he let out the breath he felt like he'd been holding for the last hour or so.

What. Had. Just. Happened?

He glanced behind him through the window of the bakery to see Charlotte deep in conversation with Steph. He couldn't interrupt her. Besides, he needed a minute.

Or ten.

Or more to digest everything that had just gone down. Not only had Charlotte totally saved his ass, she'd...*what?* Made it clear that, pretend or not, there was something between them.

If only things were different.

Amelia was fast asleep in her stroller, so instead of risking waking her by transferring her into the car, Nick decided to walk toward his new house and check on the progress. It was only a few blocks away, and the sun was warm on his face as he walked and tried—but failed—to clear his head. It was going to take a lot more to make sense of anything that had just happened in the last few hours. Still, the walk helped him calm down a little, and when he arrived at the house that was going to be his home, he couldn't help but grin.

It was going to be perfect. Close enough to Main Street that they'd be able to walk everywhere they needed. The ranch-style house backed on the river, with a huge yard and lots of trees on both sides. It would be private, and with the fence Nick was having installed, the yard would be safe for Amelia to play, even with the close proximity to the river. It was one of the bigger houses in Glacier Falls, but it was far from the grandeur of ElkView Ridge. Still, it was a million times nicer than the house Nick grew up in.

And unlike the dilapidated aluminum trailer Nick spent his childhood, this house would be a *home*. A place where Amelia could celebrate milestones, take her first steps, have birthday parties in the backyard, and most importantly, feel safe and loved. More than anything, that's all Nick wanted. He hoped like hell she would never know what it was like to feel abandoned and unloved the way he had. She'd had a rough and unfair start in life already; he'd do everything in his power to make sure that it would never happen again.

As he stood looking at the house, a truck pulled into the driveway. Travis Bishop, the contractor he'd hired, stepped out. "Hey, Nick," he said. "I didn't get an appointment wrong, did I? I didn't think we were—"

"No." Nick shook his head. "We didn't have anything lined up. I was just down the street and I thought I'd come check things out." He glanced at what he was noticing, for the first time, was a very quiet construction zone. "Are you working today? Or…"

Travis shook his head and removed the cowboy hat he wore most of the time as he approached. "Sorry, Nick. I've been up at Lynx Creek for the last few days. I told you when I took the job that I was going to have to balance things a little at least until the cabins were done, and this week…well…"

"Stephanie's back."

Travis laughed at his bluntness, but Nick wasn't stupid. He knew exactly why Travis's attentions had been on the cabins. Stephanie had hired him after a recommendation from Faith and Hope, her twin half-sisters who'd grown up in Glacier Falls, and she'd hired him first. Nick also knew that despite how sweet Steph was, she could also be pretty tough when she needed to be. Which was also why he hadn't told his friend that he'd hired her contractor for his own project.

"Say no more," Nick said. "I know how she can be."

Something flashed in Travis's eyes, but it was gone again as he replaced his hat on his head. "I think I'm figuring that out," he said.

Something about the way he said it made Nick look twice at the man. He wasn't totally oblivious, either. As preoccupied as Nick had been with his own life, he hadn't missed the way his friend flushed a little when she talked about the contractor working on her cabins, or the way they'd danced a month ago at the party Hope and Levi Langdon held for their new baby boy. There was definitely something going on between them.

"So I've been spending a bit more time over at Lynx Creek," Travis was saying. "Just finishing up on some of the details. I know Stephanie is going to have a few things she wants changed or fixed up."

"She is pretty particular," Nick agreed.

"She knows what she likes."

Doesn't she ever?

Nick had to swallow back a chuckle as he shook his head. "So what are you doing here then?"

The other man's broad smile split his face. "I'm glad you asked." He started to walk toward the garage and Nick followed, pushing the stroller. "I got notification that an order had been delivered and if it's what I think it is, I'm dying to see it for myself."

"What?"

For the life of him, Nick couldn't think of what he might have ordered for his house that would be so exciting that the man couldn't wait a few hours to see it. Of course, he wasn't a contractor.

Travis punched in the code to lift the garage door and walked straight over to a pallet that was stacked high and wrapped securely. He pulled a pocketknife from his pocket and started opening the shipment.

"I'm not going to lie, Travis. I have no idea what you're talking about. Did we order some sort of robot or something for the remodel? Because that's the only thing I can think of that would be as exciting as you're making this out to be."

Travis laughed as he sliced through the wrapping. "Sorry," he said. "I keep forgetting that not everyone gets worked up for…" He stripped back the protective materials to reveal a…window.

"Windows?"

Travis laughed. "Not just any windows, Nick. These windows block exterior hot and cold and are soundproof. They're top of the line."

Nick couldn't help but shake his head and laugh. "I've got to say, I'm glad you're so excited with them. As long as they're the best."

"They are."

"Then I'm happy." He glanced down at Amelia, who was starting to stir from her nap. "Only the best for her, okay?"

"You got it."

"Okay." He turned to leave. "I should get her home. But I totally understand it if you need to keep Stephanie happy while she's in town." He paused at his choice of words. Despite himself, he chuckled and shook his head. "Sorry, that's not

ELENA AITKEN

what I—" He looked at Travis, who was watching him with a completely unreadable expression. "Well, as far as Steph goes," he tried again. "You do what you feel is best. I can be flexible, to a point. But I am going to need a solid move-in date soon."

Remembering the meeting he'd just had only concreted his need for the house to be completed. Especially if Susan was going to *pop in* for a visit.

"I'll nail it down ASAP."

Nick started his walk home. Any sense of calm he'd had while he'd been distracted by his new home vanished the closer he got to his vehicle, and he realized for the first time what having a *pop-in* visit from his caseworker would really mean.

The one-bedroom guest house at ElkView was about to get a whole lot cozier.

"I wasn't sure if I should knock." Charlotte put her biggest, brightest smile on her face when Nick answered the door. "I mean, we are engaged to be married, right?"

After her meeting with Steph, when she'd once again remembered the predicament she'd put herself into, she'd run through a million different scenarios for how she could possibly approach things with Nick.

She didn't even know herself what she was going to say until Nick answered the door to his guest house at ElkView.

Apparently humor had won out.

It was the right choice. Nick burst into laughter and gave a shake of his head before ushering her inside. "I guess you're right," he said as she walked into the small space.

And it really was small.

Well, in comparison to her childhood bedroom that she was currently staying in, it was spacious. But for two people and a baby, especially when those two people weren't really a couple, it might as well have been one of those tiny homes that were all the rage.

A tiny home crammed with baby equipment of all kinds. Char spotted a play pen, a swing, a play mat, one of those bouncer things, a high chair, and more stuffed animals and plastic toys than she could count.

"It looks like a toy store blew up in here."

"How was your meeting with Steph?"

Char turned around and open-mouthed stared at him. "Seriously? You want to talk about that right now?"

He pulled his glasses off and pinched the bridge of his nose. It was a surprisingly endearing action and Char felt a twinge of guilt for her sarcasm.

"Yes," he said after a moment as he put his glasses back on his face. "And also, no. I mean, we have a lot to talk about, don't we?"

"Sure do." She tugged the strap of her tote bag up onto her shoulder a little higher, suddenly uncomfortable in the space. "Look, Nick. I'm really sorry—"

"I want to thank you for—"

They spoke at the same time, tripping over each other's words.

"Sorry," Char said with a smile.

"No. You go first." Nick waved toward the couch and gestured for her to sit, but Char moved instead closer to the swing where baby Amelia rocked gently, sound asleep.

"She's so sweet," she said more to herself before taking a deep breath. "I really do need to apologize, Nick." She turned around and her breath hitched in her throat. She wished she didn't have such a physical reaction to him every time she saw him. But it didn't seem to matter what he was doing or saying; it always seemed to catch her off guard a little.

"I shouldn't have jumped in like that at the coffee shop. It just...she asked who...well, it was presumptuous and risky and

I'm really sorry if I've messed everything up. I know how important Amelia is to you, and I know I don't know the situation, and it's none of my business either. But I shouldn't have done what I did and I'm really sorry." Tears pricked at her eyes as for the very first time, Charlotte realized just how reckless and damaging her behavior might have been.

She'd been selfish and stupid, and if she'd done anything to put Nick's custody arrangement in jeopardy, she'd never forgive herself. She wouldn't blame him if he was angry. No. Pissed off. Furious.

Char blinked hard and looked down at her feet, unable to make eye contact with him.

"Are you finished?" he said after a moment, a trace of humor in his question.

She nodded without looking up.

"Good," he said. "Please sit, Char. We have a lot to talk about, and I need to thank you properly."

Her head shot up. "Thank me?"

Nick nodded. "Of course. I mean, you could have given me some warning, sure. But I needed a fiancée, and you stepped up without even a second thought. That's a pretty freaking big deal. Thank you."

It was a big deal. Bigger than she'd originally thought, but...

"But honestly, I thought you were kidding about needing a wife. The other day...when I ran into you..."

He shrugged. "I wasn't really kidding."

"I guess not." But it still didn't make sense. Nick didn't seem like the type of guy to go into such an important meeting without a plan. She turned and paced toward the window. When she spun around again, he was standing directly behind her, and she almost smacked right into him. "What were you going to do? I mean, before I butted in?"

"I wish I could say I had some great plan, but there was

nothing I could do. I filed as a single man, and I was hoping my sparkling personality would win her over."

"So, I—"

"Saved me?" He grinned and shook his head all at the same time. "Are you saying my personality isn't sparkling?"

He laughed and she smiled.

Nick said she'd saved him, but maybe she screwed it all up? The thought hit her hard, and Charlotte had to force herself to take a breath. She inhaled hard and almost instantly regretted it as her senses filled with the scent of him. A combination of coffee, fresh soap, and just the tiniest trace of...baby powder. It hit her in the gut and made her stomach flip in a way that was completely inappropriate for the moment.

"I messed everything up, didn't I?"

Nick put his hands on her shoulders and squeezed gently. "Why don't we sit down and start figuring out what we're going to do and how we're going to do it." He led her to the couch and somehow Charlotte managed to nod as they sat down together. "Because no matter how we came to this place, we're here. Together."

She looked into his eyes then, and to her surprise didn't see any anger there. Only worry and concern. And was it her imagination, or was there humor there, too?

She couldn't see anything funny about the situation they were in and very quickly she was starting to regret her decision to go to Sweetie Pies early for her meeting. But maybe a little sense of humor was exactly what they needed to get them through.

It certainly couldn't hurt.

Nick had explained everything to Charlotte—well, almost everything. He didn't tell her about his concerns that Jessica might want her baby back, or the very minor but very important detail that he was 99.9% sure that Amelia wasn't even his child. Those details, although important, weren't pertinent to the immediate situation.

Besides, now that Charlotte was involved, he needed her to be fully and completely committed. If she knew that Amelia wasn't even his, well…he didn't know how she'd react. It was just easier not to say anything. Yet. He would tell her. Just not right away.

When they were done talking, Charlotte dropped her head for a moment and took in a deep breath. When she looked up, her face was set in a resolute line. "So I guess I'll be moving in."

Her matter-of-factness took him off guard, and judging by her reaction, he hadn't done a very good job of hiding it.

"Am I wrong?" She struggled to hide her smile. "Because it sounded to me like—"

"No." He stopped her. "I think that's exactly what you need to do and…soon."

"Now?"

He grinned. He did like how willing she was to accept the situation. "Now seems like a good time."

"Do you think she'd pop in right away?" Charlotte's smile fell away. "I mean, what if she was going to come right now? We'd be—"

He silenced her by putting a hand on her thigh. It felt both innocent and everything but. Her head whipped around, and she stared at him, open-mouthed, until he pulled his hand away. Instantly wishing he hadn't. He liked touching her. It felt…nice.

Under any other circumstances, Nick would have laughed at his benign choice of words for what was anything but an innocent touch. At least, it certainly didn't *feel* innocent. Not the way his heart was pounding. He jumped up from the couch, needing space before he reached out and touched her again. "We need to calm down." *In more ways than one.* "First things first. Let's get you moved in." He looked around the space. It was small. It had been small for just him and Amelia. For him, Amelia, *and* Charlotte, it was going to be downright tiny. Especially if just a simple touch from his fiancée sparked feelings in him that were anything but innocent.

"Right." Charlotte stood. "I'll go home and get a few things. I guess, I'll…"

"Do you need help? I can ask Katie to watch Amelia."

She seemed to consider his offer for a moment, but finally, she shook her head. "You know, I think it might be easier if I do it on my own." She turned to leave, but before she did, spun around again. "One thing."

"What's that?"

"Are we…well, I know it's a fake engagement and all, but… my parents are going to ask questions, and I don't think I can explain this one considering the last few months. I mean…"

Shit.

Of course. Only a few months ago, Charlotte was in a controlling relationship on the other side of the country and now she was *engaged to be married*—without even so much as a first date. Certainly her parents would have questions. Katie and Damon had kept their secret from everyone. But their situation was different. It was believable. That was a *huge* difference.

"Maybe we should just tell people the truth. I mean, only our close friends and family, not *everyone.* I think they'd understand, don't you?"

Her shrug didn't inspire much confidence, but he didn't have any other options.

"We'll just have to hope they do, won't we."

As if she sensed the stress in the air and the fact that her very future was balanced upon whether Nick and Charlotte could pull off the ultimate lie, Amelia chose that moment to wake. She let out a squawk that Nick knew would only grow louder and more insistent if he didn't respond right away. He looked from the baby back to Charlotte, and his heart swelled with a mixture of emotions he couldn't quite pin down.

Love. Hope. Fear. Gratitude. *Desire.*

He took a shaky breath, willing his emotions to stay under control. He couldn't lose his grip now. He squeezed his eyes shut for a second, giving himself a moment to pull it together before going to the baby. If he was worked up, she'd feel it. And the last thing he needed on top of everything else was for Amelia to get worked up, too.

His eyes flew open a moment later when Charlotte wrapped her arms around him and squeezed. He jumped a little, but she held him tighter.

A hug.

The physical touch almost broke the thin thread he had on his control. But the longer she held him, the better he started to feel, until he unwound his arms and returned the embrace.

She smelled of lemons and vanilla.

"We've got this, Nick," she murmured into his ear. "It'll be okay."

Simple words. But, somehow, coming from Charlotte with her arms around him, he believed them.

Chapter Seven

CHARLOTTE WASN'T NAIVE ENOUGH to think that her parents wouldn't have something to say about it when she told them she'd be moving in with Nick Newton, Glacier Fall's newest billionaire resident. Which was why she'd decided to go with the truth when it came to trying to explain what she was doing. Her mom and dad had been her rock for far too long to lead with a lie now.

And fortunately for Charlotte, their capacity to be understanding was even greater than she'd expected.

"You're a grown woman," Darlene said. "We're not going to tell you what to do." She sat on Char's bed and picked up a T-shirt, folding it neatly into thirds before picking another out of the pile Charlotte had dumped there. "But I really do hope you know what you're doing."

"I'm helping Nick, Mom." Char picked her favorite pairs of jeans out of the drawer and put them in the suitcase. She was trying to decide how much to take. Enough to make it look like she actually lived there, but not too much that there was nowhere to put any of it. She hadn't inspected the bedroom when she'd been there earlier, but she wasn't confident that there was much space. "If you were to see him with his daughter, you'd understand why I had to do it."

"And he didn't ask you…"

Char knew that would be the hardest part for her mom to understand. How Charlotte had just recklessly jumped into the situation without so much as a discussion about it beforehand.

"I know it sounds crazy, Mom. But in that moment, there was no other choice. I knew he needed help and if it meant him losing Amelia to…" She realized she didn't fully understand what the consequence of Nick not having a fiancée would be. *Would custody go to Amelia's mother? Was there someone else interested in custody? What if she hadn't stepped in?*

There was a lot she didn't know. So many questions she still needed answers to.

But it looked as though she'd have the opportunity to figure it out if they were going to be spending so much time together.

"And how long are you going to be there? A week, you said?"

"I didn't say." She raised an eyebrow in her mother's direction. "Look, Mom, I know you're worried, but honestly, I'm doing fine. Nick is just a friend." But the word didn't sound right. Not really. Sure, he was a friend, but was he more? Or maybe the better question was, *could* he be more? She shook her head and forced herself to focus. "You always taught me to look after my friends."

"I did, but this is—"

"Not different," she interrupted. "Not at all. I know you'll understand when you meet Nick and Amelia. How about we set up a dinner or something once everything is settled a bit? Would that make you feel better?"

Her mother nodded.

"I'm not sure when, but I'll arrange it." She smiled at the idea of her mom meeting Amelia. Char just knew she'd melt at the little girl's giggle, just the way she had. Amelia was abso-

lutely impossible not to fall head over heels for. *As for her father…*
She blushed at the thought of falling for him. Or maybe she
already was.

"Char?"

"Sorry." She blinked as she realized she'd totally missed
whatever her mother had just said. "What were you saying?"

Her mother gave her a strange look. "I was just wondering
if this meant you might want to come into the office now
instead of working from home? You know, that way we can see
you a bit more."

The office?

Oh.

Guilt filled her as she realized that with everything that had
happened, she'd forgotten to tell her mother that the meeting
with Stephanie Starz had gone well. *Really* well, in fact. On an
ordinary day, she would have run right home to tell her mother
all about it and celebrate with her. But…the day had been
anything but ordinary.

"I totally forgot. I had that meeting with Stephanie Starz
and—"

"You *forgot?*" Her mother's mouth fell open and Char
couldn't help but laugh. "This Nick must really be something
else if he made you forget about the biggest meeting you've
ever had in what could be the biggest move in your career."

He was.

But she didn't say that. Instead, Charlotte smiled and filled
her mom in on how well the meeting had gone, including how
Stephanie had loved all of Char's ideas and even had a few of
her own to add before offering her the contract: all of the
cabins at Lynx Creek, including a purchasing budget that
Charlotte could only ever have dreamed of working with
before. The money she made from the project would not only
be enough to move out on her own, but it should be enough for
a down payment on a small house in town.

Darlene, as Char knew she would be, was stunned and thrilled for her daughter. "I'm sad you won't be working for us anymore," she said when she'd finished letting out whoops of joy. "I know it's not what you want to do, but I have to admit I've kind of liked having you around so much again, and I'm going to miss you."

A tear formed in her mother's eye, and Char immediately pulled her into a hug.

"Don't cry! I'm not going anywhere, Mom. It's not like I'm moving far or getting married or anything. I'm literally going to be ten minutes away and I was thinking…"

Her mom wiped her eyes.

"I wasn't sure you'd go for this or not," Char started. "And I'm going to be pretty busy with Lynx Creek, but…well, I was thinking maybe I could offer you some staging services to your real estate clients." She continued before her mother could object. "I know it's not usually done here, but in the bigger markets, they use stagers to make the house look as good as possible before the photos are taken. After seeing some of your clients' places, I think maybe it's a service that is necessary. Especially with the market getting more and more competitive."

Char bit her bottom lip while she let her mother process what she'd just said. She really hoped she wouldn't take it as an insult, and only as a constructive suggestion.

To her surprise, Darlene nodded and laughed. "You know what, I think that's a very good idea. Especially if you're a consultant. Then it's not like I'm telling my clients to clean up after themselves—you can do it."

"Something like that." Char laughed and shook her head. "We can talk about it. But for now I should probably get going back to ElkView for dinner."

Her mom and dad helped her out to the car with her few bags and a box full of framed photos her mother had grabbed from various surfaces around the house to "Make it look like you live there."

And she was on her way.

In less than twenty-four hours, her career had taken a huge leap forward *and* she'd gained a fiancé.

It had been quite a day. Charlotte was exhausted but also, she'd never felt quite so energized.

"You guys can totally pull this off." Katie set a wooden bowl full of salad on the table and put a teething biscuit in front of Amelia in her high chair before sitting down with the rest of them.

When Damon had popped over to invite Nick for dinner, and found Charlotte awkwardly unpacking her things, he'd quickly amended his invitation to include Nick's new fiancée as well. Nick knew they were putting off the inevitable discussions they were most certainly going to have in length, but he didn't see the harm in a little social intervention first. Particularly because Katie and Damon were the experts in fake relationships.

"I hope you're right." Nick reached for a piece of pizza that Damon had just brought from the outdoor pizza oven. It was a warm spring night, so they'd decided to eat on the patio while Damon tended to the pizzas in his custom-made outdoor oven, his latest addition. "I mean, I can't even think about—"

"So don't," Charlotte cut him off. "Don't think about what *could* happen," she amended. "Because Katie's right. We can totally pull this off. There's no reason why we can't."

Nick could think of a few, not the least of which was that they weren't really a couple. But his negativity wasn't going to do any of them any good. He pushed it aside and focused solely on the positive outcome: Amelia legally being his daughter. That was the only outcome he could envision. *Laser focus.*

He smiled at his baby, who sucked and gnawed on the biscuit Katie had given her.

"But there are a few things you'll have to sort out first," Katie said.

"Oh yeah," Damon added as he took his seat across from Nick. "Like how you're going to manage…" He waved his finger between Nick and Char.

"What is…" Nick mimicked his action.

Damon's laugh was cocky. He leaned back in his chair and put his arm around his wife. "This attraction the two of you have."

"What?" Char almost choked on her pizza.

Nick quickly poured her a glass of water and handed it to her, before turning to glare at his *best friend.*

Damon simply shrugged, but Katie pushed his arm off her shoulders.

"Seriously," Katie said. "You are not subtle."

"I never said anything about subtle." He picked up a piece of pizza and took a big bite. "But you see it, too," Damon said through a full mouth. "You know I'm right."

Attraction?

Nick couldn't even pretend that he wasn't attracted to Charlotte. Of course he was. He was a man, and she was a gorgeous woman. She was also sweet, and funny, and smart, and…*shit. Yes.* There was definitely an attraction. And that kiss…such a sweet, innocent kiss that had been *so* much more. He glanced in her direction. She'd recovered from the near choking, but her face was flushed pink.

Was she attracted to him, too?

Was it more than a friendship?

And if it was…what did that mean?

"I mean, you are going to be sharing a bed," Damon

continued, either completely unaware that he was stirring a pot that was already simmering, or fully aware and loving it. "It's a small place and if they said they're going to—"

"Damon!" Katie smacked his arm lightly and shot him a look, but her husband seemed unaffected.

"What? I'm not wrong."

He wasn't and Nick said as much.

"It's actually a good point," Nick said, adding quickly, "Even if your approach is screwed up."

Damon grinned as if it were a compliment.

"But it is a small place and the new house won't be ready for a little while yet. We're going to have to figure out how to—"

"We'll have to share the bed."

Nick was thankful he was seated at the table because his body reacted immediately and unexpectedly at her comment. He looked at Char, who was no longer blushing and instead looked matter-of-fact.

"It's the only real solution," she commented. "I mean, Susan did say the visits were unscheduled to make sure they caught us in our natural environment, right? It wouldn't look good if she caught me sleeping on the couch or—"

"I'd be sleeping on the couch," Nick corrected her. "I'd never let you sleep on the couch."

Her smile was sweet. "The point is, neither of us should be sleeping on the couch."

True.

Nick's head was a mess. The conversation naturally drifted into other subjects as Katie started asking Charlotte questions about the Lynx Creek cabins and advice for the redecorating she was hoping to do herself. Nick was grateful for her distraction because he needed to calm down whatever was going on inside him. From the moment he'd met Charlotte, he'd been attracted to her, sure. But this was different. The feelings suddenly shooting through him, and sparking a flame of desire that he hadn't felt since Amelia had been brought into his life, were unexpected. Well, not entirely unexpected. But he was completely unprepared for them.

But now that they'd been sparked, there was no way to put out the flame. Every time she spoke, or looked at him, it flared up again.

He needed to get control over that, and quickly, because there was only one goal here, and it didn't involve any other female besides the one who was currently smashing her now soggy biscuit into her chair and squealing with glee at the mess she was making.

Yes, Amelia was his focus. There was no room for distractions of any kind.

But…

———

"What side of the bed do you sleep on?" Charlotte stood at the bottom of the bed and assessed the situation that they'd tried to avoid for the last few hours.

After dinner with Katie and Damon, which had been both fun and stressful for entirely different reasons, they'd returned to the guest house, put Amelia down for the night, and tried to kill as much time as possible in the living room talking over some of the *details* of their relationship and subsequent engagement before finally Charlotte couldn't stop yawning and there was no more putting it off.

They needed to go to bed.

Together.

"A side?" Nick appeared fresh from the bathroom, smelling like peppermint toothpaste, at her side.

"Yes. A side." She looked at him and her heart did a strange skipping thing in her chest. It was late, and rough stubble covered his chin. His thick hair was tousled and he'd left his glasses in the bathroom. He looked…sexy as hell. She tried to ignore the fact that he only wore pajama bottoms, that hung a little lower on his hips than would be considered appropriate for any other situation besides sleeping. Never mind his bare chest that showed the long, lean muscles he kept hidden under his clothing.

Charlotte swallowed hard and looked away. "Everyone has a side they sleep on. What's yours?"

"I don't believe in sides," he said. "You pick."

She shook her head. *Everyone* had a side. "I sleep on the left."

"Works for me." Nick moved to the corner of the room where the crib was set up and Amelia was fast asleep. He tucked a blanket around her and bent to kiss her on the forehead. Charlotte's heart fluttered in her chest, watching the sweet interaction, but she forced herself to look away and climb into the bed. On the left side.

She laid on her side and stared at the wall, forcing herself to relax enough so she could sleep, although she had no idea how she was going to manage that. She felt the mattress dip as Nick, too, climbed into bed. Damon's accusation at dinner, that they were attracted to each other, kept replaying in her head on repeat. Neither of them had denied it. She didn't know about Nick, but she'd be straight-up lying if she said she wasn't attracted to him. It had been a slow build, but it was definitely growing in intensity with every second that went by. And the fact that he was only inches away, half naked, in the same bed, wasn't helping.

Maybe it would be best to just address it. Get it out of the way so they could just stop dancing around it and move on?

It couldn't hurt.

Well, at least it couldn't make things any more awkward than they already were.

Char took a breath, rolled over to her other side, and almost smacked directly into Nick's face.

Why was he so close?

"Oh, you're right here."

"Am I too far over?"

She couldn't help it, Charlotte burst out laughing and immediately clamped a hand over her mouth to stifle the sound when she remembered the baby was sleeping only a few feet away.

"Oops."

"She can sleep through anything." Nick was grinning too, and he'd made no move to give her space.

Did he want to be close to her, too?

If she'd wanted to, all she had to do was lean in an inch or so and her lips would be on his.

If she wanted to.

And did she want to?

Easy answer.

Yes.

Her entire body thrummed with his nearness and the fact that they were lying in a bed together. And of course there was the small detail that he was half naked.

Oh yes. She wanted to.

The desire surprised her. Not because she wasn't attracted to Nick; she was. But because there'd been a time not all that long ago when she couldn't have possibly considered that she'd ever be attracted to another man again. Not in a serious way. And definitely not in a way that she'd actually want to do something about. Billy had destroyed her self-esteem and turned her into a person she didn't recognize, and frankly, one she didn't like all that much.

But she'd worked through a lot. Lauren was an amazing therapist, and Char wasn't the same woman who'd returned to Glacier Falls with her tail tucked between her legs. Not even close. In fact, she wasn't even the same woman she was before she'd moved to be with Billy.

She was stronger. She was smarter and, most importantly, she was becoming the type of woman who was true to herself and was finally giving herself permission to live the life she deserved.

Which was exactly why she was currently in Nick Newton's bed, only inches away from him, staring very directly into his sexy, dark eyes.

"Can you even see without your glasses?"

His lips twitched up in a smile. "I can see you perfectly. I'm nearsighted." The hand he'd had tucked under the pillow came out and one finger touched her nose lightly. "See? That's your nose."

She laughed. "You could see my nose a mile away. It's huge."

"It's perfect."

Her breath caught in her throat.

Nick watched her closely, his finger still touching her nose.

She swallowed hard.

Her thoughts bounced all over, unable to focus on just one thing. Not that she could blame herself. It had been a crazy few hours. Since waking up that morning, she now had herself a sexy billionaire for a fiancé, had moved into his house, *and* as if it couldn't get any more complicated, had learned through one super innocent kiss that she was insanely sexually attracted to her fiancé. And now she was lying only inches from him in his bed.

Yup. There were a few things going on in her brain.

But even with all the craziness going on, the number-one thought she couldn't seem to shut off was just how much she wanted to kiss him again.

"Char?"

She nodded and swallowed hard.

"Can I tell you the truth?"

"Of course."

"I actually think you're gorgeous."

Her mouth opened and shut, with no words coming out.

So much for strong and smart.

"I know this is complicated," he continued.

"That's an understatement."

He smiled and trailed his finger down to her cheek. "And I know you've gone through a lot lately and with Amelia…well, I need you to know that she's my focus."

"Of course she is," she said, without addressing what she'd gone through. "That's why I'm here."

"This isn't coming out right." He inhaled slowly before releasing his breath. His finger trailed down her face and traced the outline of her lips. "When you kissed me earlier… well…I know this is going to sound stupid."

Char's breath caught in her throat. "I don't think it will."

His smile was sweet, but there was heat behind it, too, when he said, "It was the most incredible kiss I've ever had."

"That doesn't sound stupid at all."

"It doesn't?"

She shook her head. "It was the best kiss I've ever had, too."

"Really?" He shifted closer to her, and she nodded.

It was hard to breathe with him touching her. With him so close. With him saying the things he was saying.

"And I want you to know that what Damon said earlier… he wasn't wrong."

Damon wasn't wrong.

"No," she said so softly, she almost couldn't hear herself. "He wasn't wrong."

He moved even closer so she could feel his breath on her lips. "So what do we do?"

For Char, there was one clear answer, but it wasn't that easy and she knew it. Still… "I'd like to kiss you again."

His lips curved up in a smile. "I like the sound of that."

She did too. *So* much. She shut her eyes as he closed the tiny distance between them, but before his lips touched hers, he stopped.

"Char?"

Her eyes popped open.

"I can't promise you anything right now."

"I know."

"Amelia is—"

"I know." She stopped him. "Like I said, that's why I'm here."

But it wasn't the only reason she was there. And that became crystal-clear to her when, a moment later, Nick cupped her cheek with his hand and pressed his lips to hers in a kiss that erased any lingering hesitations either of them might've had.

And that meant she was in trouble. Because whether she planned it or not, things had just become a whole lot more complicated.

Chapter Eight

FROM THE MOMENT Stephanie had seen the Lynx Creek property, she knew it was special. And every single time she came back to Glacier Falls and saw the progress Travis Bishop had made, she got a little more excited. She hated to admit it—least of all to him, because his head would only get even bigger than it already was—but the man was damn good at what he did.

After her meeting with Charlotte Davis, Stephanie had gone directly to Ever After Ranch to see her sisters and even more importantly, her new baby nephew, Cole. By the time she'd returned to Lynx Creek for the night, it had been late and she'd been exhausted and in no state to check out the process on construction, even if there had been any daylight left.

But with the dawning of a new day, and a coffee in hand, Steph was ready to go exploring.

Her cabin, Bankside, had been the first one Travis had restored. She knew from his last email that he'd recently finished up with a few of the cabins farther up in the trees, so she set off on the trail that led toward them. Overhead, the trees were alive with the sounds of all types of birds that had recently returned from their migration. Steph let the sweet sounds fill her and block out any lingering stress she'd been feeling from being in LA.

There'd been a time when she'd enjoyed the business of the big city, but more and more she longed for the peace and quiet of the forest and the mountains. Certainly, her sister Faith would make some sort of quip about her getting old, and she was probably right.

She didn't want to say that her clock was ticking, because that wasn't it. With baby Cole and Amelia in her life, she didn't feel any strong pull to have children of her own. At least not yet. But she couldn't help but be envious of her friends who surrounded her with their happily ever afters. It seemed like every time she turned around, someone else was finding their soul mate and falling desperately in love. Since her failed engagement, which ended up in a very public and somewhat embarrassing break-up, she hadn't had any prospects at all.

Travis Bishop.

No. Travis was absolutely not a prospect.

No way.

Sure, he was ridiculously gorgeous...if you liked that strong, silent, slightly broody, way too cocky for their own good, cowboy type.

Which apparently she did.

But even if she was ridiculously physically attracted to him, it would never happen.

He'd made that more than clear.

Just remembering the way they'd almost kissed, her so sure he was attracted to her as she was to him, only to have him more or less shove her away as if she were disgusting, was enough to remind her that, no, it would never happen.

Ever.

Annoyed that thoughts of Travis had affected her forest

zen, Steph shook it off and did her best to refocus on the beauty that surrounded her.

Before she got to the little cabin that was the farthest away from her own and the most secluded, she stopped and gazed out at the view that the ridge afforded her.

Stunning: the mountains, the forest...all of it. It never failed to take her breath away and give her the feeling of home.

Steph had grown up in a town a few hours north of Glacier Falls. It was also full of forest and snow, from what she could remember. In fact, beyond her parents—who were the most amazing, loving parents she could have ever hoped for—Steph didn't have much in the way of positive memories of her hometown. It was one of the reasons she was so excited to move away and start a new life when she was twenty. And that's exactly what she did. She wasn't looking to be a celebrity or a movie star. Not at all. She had wanted to be an advertising executive.

Steph laughed at herself now when she thought that she might ever be good at marketing in any way, but when she was in college, she was convinced that it was the most glamorous of jobs. Fortunately for her, she'd been a student at the University of British Columbia and working part-time at a coffee shop to make ends meet when a talent agent shooting a new series in the area ordered a venti, extra hot, no foam, extra whip mocha. Steph handed him the drink and the next thing she knew, she was being pulled into a meeting with a producer.

It really had all happened just that fast.

Stephanie had ended up replacing the star of that series—a young woman with a drug problem—and after four seasons, her celebrity was concreted. She'd forgotten about school and had instead poured herself into the entertainment industry. She'd moved from one starring role to another, and it didn't take long before she was one of Hollywood's highest-paid actresses. And she had the reputation of being the best to work with. She was unstoppable.

And she wasn't complaining.

Stephanie loved her life.

Or at least, she had.

It wasn't that she didn't love it anymore. She just wanted more.

It was time.

With her eyes closed, she inhaled deeply. Maybe the forest air would give her the answers she sought.

A rustling in the bushes behind her spooked her. She dropped her coffee mug and fell to her knees as she turned around to see what it was.

If it were a bear, she should run.

No. Maybe that was a cougar.

Yes. A cougar, you run. A bear, you fight.

Or maybe it was the other way around.

Shit.

She really needed to brush up on some basic survival skills if she was going to live out here on her own.

The rustling got louder as the creature grew closer, until it —barked.

It was more of a woof than a bark. But still.

Steph tilted her head and tried to see through the dense bushes that were just starting to leaf out, at whatever it was that was startling her.

"Hello?" she called, her voice still thin and shaky. "Who are —oh." A smile split her face. "You're a puppy." Steph knelt on the dirt path and held out her hand. "It's okay. I won't—"

The puppy bounded out of the bush and straight into her, knocking her flat on her back as she licked Steph's face. She was still giggling and wrestling with the remarkably large bundle of fur a few minutes later when she heard the familiar voice that never failed to spark something inside her.

"I see you found Tinker Bell."

Steph took a moment to compose herself, a feat that was virtually impossible considering she was lying on her back, with a giant puppy on her chest licking her face. Still laughing, somehow she managed to slip out from under the dog and sit up.

She almost regretted it the second she made eye contact with Travis. And a shot of desire ran through her, settling in her core.

Damn, he looked good.

He always looked good. *Really* good. But from this angle, he looked downright sinful in his shorts and…nothing else.

Seriously. Where *was* his shirt?

It was beyond frustrating that she was so ridiculously attracted to the man. Especially considering he went out of his way to avoid her and on the few occasions they did find themselves in close proximity, he couldn't get away fast enough.

"Tinker Bell?" She managed to speak the word as he offered her a hand to help her up. "You named a giant dog after a tiny fairy?"

She ignored his hand and pushed herself to standing. Stephanie ignored his grin.

"She's not giant now," he said. "Besides, I found her in a patch of the purple flowers."

"What do crocuses have to do with fairies?" She focused on his eyes so she wouldn't have to look at his chest, which was smooth, ripped, and way too tanned considering it was only April. She swallowed hard.

"Nothing." He shrugged. "I was just testing you to see if you knew what they were called."

"You don't think I know my flowers?"

"I don't know what you know."

"I know a lot of things. I think you'd be impressed."

She didn't mean for it to sound flirty or sexual at all, but when he narrowed his eyes and dipped his head a little and said, "Oh, I have no doubt of that," Steph was certain she was going to completely self-combust.

She had to get control of her emotions. One man should not have the ability to impact her so dramatically and it was getting beyond annoying. Especially because he was just playing with her. No doubt because he could. Travis Bishop was exactly like every overconfident boy she used to know growing up who thought they were God's gift to women. Cocky and arrogant and—

"Where is your shirt?" She blurted out the question and he laughed.

"Why? Am I distracting you?"

Steph inhaled deeply in an effort to stay in control of the spiraling situation. "Yes," she answered honestly. "You look cold."

He laughed harder. "I'm not cold. I was out for a run."

That would explain the glistening.

"A run? But...don't you live..." She realized she had no idea where he lived. She really didn't know anything about Travis at all except that he was sexy as sin and made her feel things she wasn't even sure were possible.

He roughed his hair with his hand and squatted down to pet the dog, who was tugging on the laces of his runners. "I'm living in my vehicle right now."

"What?"

"Don't get all worked up." He looked up at her and grinned.

She liked him at this angle, too.

"It's not nearly as pathetic as it sounds. A few years back, I refitted an old bus to be a camper. It's actually really comfortable with pretty much all the comforts of home, only…"

"It's not a home."

He stood and crossed his arms over his chest. "No," he agreed. "It's not a home. But it'll do for now."

"How long have you been living in a *van?*"

He cocked an eyebrow. "It's not a *van*. It's a camper. And not long. I was living on the Langdon ranch while I was working there, but when the Langdons sold, I decided to stay in the camper until I figured out where I wanted to build. So this made sense."

Stephanie couldn't imagine how living in a van or a bus or whatever it was made any sense at all, but for Travis…maybe it did. She really shouldn't be surprised by anything anymore. "Okay, so if you're living in a *camper* and you're out for a run so early, does that mean—"

"I'm not living on your property," he interrupted before she could finish. "If that's what you're going to ask."

"I was…not that I'd care…"

"You wouldn't?" He grinned and took a step toward her. "Really?"

Was that a challenge? What was it with this man? Why did he push all of her buttons as if it were a game? It probably was to him.

Fortunately, before she had to answer, or he could get any closer, Tinker Bell, tired of being ignored, let out a bark at her feet. She bent down and gave the black and white fluff ball attention until she started licking her face and trying to clamber up on her. When she stood again, Travis was still standing close, watching her.

"You have a little…" He reached out and used his thumb to wipe something from her cheek.

She couldn't control her reaction, but she closed her eyes and sucked in a breath at his touch. It was as if he'd left a trail of fire on her skin.

"It's just mud," he said and she snapped her eyes open.

He was even closer now. Only inches away. Close enough that she could smell the woodsiness of him mixed with the sharp tang of his physical exertion. It was the sexiest scent she'd ever experienced. His eyes darkened and he didn't move away to give either of them space. Unlike every other time, he wasn't pushing her away. Trying to control her breathing was a losing battle. When he finally cupped her cheek with the same hand he'd just wiped the mud away with, Steph was pretty sure she'd stopped breathing altogether.

She was sure he was going to kiss her. But she'd been sure before, and...by the time she was able to process what had actually happened, Travis released her and took a step back.

She expected to see the usual cockiness reflected in his eyes, but there was no trace of it. Instead, he looked...confused.

But only for a moment before he recovered from whatever it was that had just happened between them. "I should finish up my run."

She nodded dumbly.

"And just so you know, not that it matters, but I own the property on the other side of the river. We're neighbors. That's where I'm living."

Neighbors?

He turned and disappeared down the trail. At her feet, Tinker Bell let out a sharp bark and took off after him, leaving Stephanie to try to process what just happened.

It wasn't until after they were both long gone and she could once again hear the birds in the trees overhead that she realized she hadn't even asked about his work on her cabins.

Chapter Nine

IT WAS COMPLICATED.

No. Nick mentally corrected himself.

It was way more than complicated.

Especially considering Char didn't even know the truth that he wasn't Amelia's father. Now that the dust had settled with everything that happened the day before, with her just jumping in to help him, no questions asked, that seemed like a *really* important detail that she deserved to know.

And then there was the kiss.

Somehow, he'd managed to get some sleep the night before after they'd kissed.

That's all they'd done. But it had been enough.

Enough to turn an already twisted situation into a complete cluster of complication.

Which he shouldn't have done.

He needed to keep his focus on Amelia and making sure they didn't screw that up with this fake relationship that had some very real feelings. And real feelings were exactly where the problems started.

A relationship of any kind could only make things worse.

What if things didn't work out or they had an argument or…what if it screwed things up with his adoption? He couldn't risk it. Amelia was the most important consideration. No matter how he was feeling about Charlotte.

And he *was* feeling something for her. Oh, was he ever.

Nick knew he was playing with fire when he'd gotten into the bed the night before, far closer than he should have. Maybe they had to sleep in the same bed, but he could have been a gentleman and scooted to the far edge. But he hadn't. Like a magnet, he'd been drawn close to her. *Really* close.

He should have turned away. He shouldn't have told her he was attracted to her. He…it didn't matter. It had happened. And *damn*—that kiss and the one after that had been fire. He'd thought the tiny, chaste kiss in the coffee shop had been amazing. But their kisses the night before had been absolutely life changing.

And now, in the light of the new morning, with Charlotte still fast asleep only inches from him, Nick was going to have to…*what?*

He laid back on his pillow and stared straight up at the ceiling.

What? What was he going to do?

He knew what he *wanted* to do. But was it the right thing?

And first things first. Before it went any further, he needed to tell her the truth.

"Good morning."

He flipped over to see Charlotte watching him.

"Hi." He couldn't help but smile at the sight of her. She was so damn beautiful. Especially first thing in the morning. "How long have you been up?"

"Long enough to see that something is bothering you."

He blinked hard. "I wouldn't say *bothering* me. But…yeah, okay." He scrubbed a hand over his face. "I need to tell you something."

Her smile faded a little, but Nick pressed on.

"I need you to know that I'm not biologically Amelia's father."

"What?" She sat up a little, propped up on an elbow. "I don't—"

"I mean, I *am* her father." He cut her off. "When she was dropped off with me, I wasn't sure but it didn't take long for me to figure it out. But by the time I did, I was already completely smitten with her and there was no way I could let Amelia go into the system and…"

"Hey." She put a hand on his arm to still him. "It's okay."

"It's okay?" He blinked.

"Well…" She shrugged a little. "I'm not going to lie. I'm surprised. *Very* surprised. But I've seen you with Amelia, and I can see how much you love her. What about her mother? You've never said anything about her."

Nick took a deep breath and told Charlotte everything he knew about Jessica. Including how he'd hired a private investigator to look into her situation. He told her that he'd wanted everyone to think Amelia was his, but only a few people knew the truth. He even told Charlotte how he'd told Stephanie that he'd called off the private investigator, only to hire him again. And because he was telling the truth, he also let her know about how he'd grown up with an addict mother and refused to let Amelia experience that lifestyle as well.

"It makes sense," Charlotte said when he was finished explaining. "I understand."

"You do?"

She laughed a little. "How could I not?"

"And you still want to help me out even though I didn't tell you the truth?"

Her smile was so warm, it instantly made Nick feel better.

"Of course," she said. "In fact, it kind of makes me want to help you out even more. Biology aside, Amelia *is* your daughter. I'll do anything I can to make sure you get custody of her. She belongs with you."

"I can't even tell you how happy I am to hear that." Relief washed through him. But that wasn't the only complication he needed to address this morning. There was the whole matter of the kiss. Only, he really didn't want to talk about that. Because what he really wanted to do was kiss her again. It took all his willpower not to reach out and pull her close. "There's one more thing we should probably talk about," he said. "About last night—"

"Nick, what we did…the kiss…I'm really—"

"No." It suddenly became critically important that she did not apologize for the kiss or try to dismiss it in any way. If she did that, he didn't know if he'd be able to reconcile it in his head. Because… "No," he said again. "Don't apologize or… just…" He shook his head. "I meant what I said last night," he said, deciding on the path of least resistance. "I *am* attracted to you, Char. And I also can't promise you anything. Not right now. Amelia has to—"

"She has to be your first priority," she interrupted and finished for him. "I know. You said that." She smiled. "A few times. And I understand. Don't worry about me, okay? I'm a big girl. This isn't serious. This isn't real."

Her words, although completely true, sent a stab to his heart. It sure felt real and serious. But she was right. She had to be.

He nodded.

"So…I'm okay with that if you are," she finished. "Besides, I'm not looking for anything right now anyway."

That made sense after what she'd been through, but again…her words hit him hard, and he didn't like the way they made him feel inside.

"So what are you saying?" Nick desperately wanted to touch her. She was so close to him, but at the same time the distance between them was too much. Still lying on his side, propped up by one arm, he reached his free hand out to touch hers.

"Well…"

She gave him a sassy grin that made him want to flip her on her back and kiss her senseless. Instead, he swallowed hard and fought the urge while she finished her thought.

"If we're affectionate, it can only make things look more credible, right? I mean, if Susan were to stop by or see us at the store or something."

He nodded.

"So…why don't we just not worry about complicated or any of that? I know Amelia is your priority, and I don't want anything serious." She shrugged. "It seems pretty perfect to me."

It did to him, too. If it meant being able to kiss her again and not put his custody at risk, there didn't seem to be anything wrong with her plan at all.

"I can't disagree with that."

"So we're in agreement?"

He bent and sealed their agreement with a kiss.

Without taking his lips from hers, Nick moved so he was over top of her and able to deepen the kiss the way he yearned to.

Complicated was the furthest thing from his mind when she let out a small moan and wrapped her arms around his back. There was nothing complicated about what he was feeling at that exact moment. Nothing at all.

"Charlotte." Her name came out on a deep breath. "I know we…I…"

She reached down, pulled him back to her, and it was Nick's turn to moan.

Oh yes, it was going to be an absolutely perfect arrangement.

A sound that was half screech-half laugh came from the corner of the room, and Nick jumped back, off Charlotte. It was so abrupt that he couldn't help but burst out laughing. A moment later, he heard Charlotte join in with his laughter and from her crib, Amelia, too, squealed her delight.

He hauled himself from the bed, but allowed himself one last look at Char, still lying in the blankets, looking even more gorgeous than she had a few minutes ago, because now her lips were reddened from their kiss, the memory of her on his own lips. "I guess Amelia has other ideas about how we should be spending our morning."

"To be continued then." She winked and rolled over to slip out of her side of the bed.

Nick couldn't be sure if it was the lingering effects of the kiss, the sight of her ass in her pajama shorts—that even without his glasses, he could see clearly—or the very clear promise of *later*, or all of the above, but suddenly *complicated* was no longer an issue. The idea of anything happening with Charlotte being anything but amazing was the furthest thing from his mind.

"Okay, wait." Jeremy spun around and walked back toward where Charlotte sat.

She'd asked her brother to meet her in the park by the waterfalls in town because it would definitely be better to break the news about her *engagement* in a public place. Her brother was the most supportive man she knew, next to her father, but he also had the tendency to be more than a little overprotective. And she was pretty sure he wouldn't understand why she'd jumped into an engagement with a man she barely knew—fake or not.

"So…" He came to a stop in front of the picnic table Char was perched upon. "You're engaged?"

She nodded.

"To Nick Newton?"

She nodded again.

"The billionaire single dad?"

"Yup," she said. "That's pretty much the gist of it." She grinned and then quickly added, "But it's not real. Don't forget that part."

"Right…" He ran a hand through his hair, making it stand up in odd angles. "And you're not dating? Just friends?"

She opened her mouth to answer, but closed it again. Were they friends? Yes. But that kiss earlier this morning was definitely more than friendly. *Much more.* But they'd made it very clear that there was not going to be anything serious between them. She'd made sure of that with her little white lie. Well, it wasn't *really* a lie. She wasn't looking for anything serious. She'd just come out of a terrible relationship and she had been looking forward to being single again and rebuilding her life. That was all true. Very true. But…when she kissed Nick, there was nothing casual about it. He made her want things she didn't know she even wanted again.

Still, Amelia was the focus and she knew that. So she'd told him what they both needed to hear.

"It's complicated."

She almost laughed out loud at the choice of word. It was an understatement to be sure, and she was getting really tired of the word altogether.

"Complicated?" Jeremy scoffed. "That's the stupidest cop-out I've ever heard. Complicated." He drew out the word until it sounded ridiculous. "You might as well say that you have commitment issues."

Char did laugh out loud at that. "I don't think that's the problem here," she said. "After all, we are engaged."

Jeremy glared at her, turned around, and walked back toward the fence to look out over the falls. "I don't like it," he said after a moment. "A fake engagement is never a good idea and—"

"Jeremy?"

He turned around and Char shrugged. "I don't really care if you like it or not." She may have been the older sister, but Jeremy had been the protective one as long as she could remember. She almost never discounted his opinion, but there was a time for everything. "Because I'm doing it. I'm just letting you know because you're my brother, and I love you." She stood and jumped down from the table. "But I'm not asking you permission."

Jeremy looked as though he were going to object, but instead he just dropped his gaze to the ground and shook his head. "What about Billy?"

"Billy?" She took a step back, anger flaring in her. "What about Billy? This has nothing to do with him."

"Doesn't it?"

Char clenched her fists at her sides and released them slowly. He was only trying to wind her up, she knew that. She just didn't know why. "It doesn't," she said slowly and took a breath. "I know you're trying to look out for me, Jer, but I'm not a little girl anymore and—"

"Char, I just had to *save* you from a shitty situation." He moved to stand close enough that Charlotte could see the worry lines on his face. "I can't stand by and watch you fall into another one."

"Nick isn't like Billy. It's totally different. And it's not like we're...well...it's just different." It was a lame explanation, but there was no way she was about to tell her brother that even though it was a fake engagement, her feelings for Nick were growing every day. And quickly. No. It definitely wasn't the time to mention that.

"But you're not ready."

"Excuse me?" Char froze and stared at her brother. "I love you, Jeremy, but you do not have any right to tell me if I'm ready to help out a friend, or get involved in a new relationship, or anything of the sort. I've been working hard with my therapist, not that it's any of your business. Billy was a mistake. Yes. A big one. And that whole stage of my life has changed me, but it will *not* define me." Her voice rose; it trembled a bit as she worked to control her escalating emotions. "You're my brother, and I care about you and your opinion, but unless and until I ask for it, keep it to yourself."

Jeremy opened his mouth and Charlotte braced herself for whatever it was he was about to say. Finally, he closed it and looked at his feet with a shake of his head. "I knew I couldn't trust that guy," he muttered. "Just be careful, Char. Because I don't…well, never mind."

"Thank you."

She knew it was hard for him to swallow his opinion. *Really* hard. But she appreciated his effort.

Jeremy kicked at a rock. "And…you're okay?" he asked. "I mean, everything else? Billy hasn't tried to—"

"Nope. Nothing." She cut him off quickly because she knew what he was going to ask. The same thing he always asked her: Had Billy contacted her? It seemed almost unfathomable that she'd fled that relationship and had never heard from him again. She'd literally left with nothing because she just wanted to get out. And not once had she heard from him. Until recently.

Well, she wasn't sure it *was* Billy. But a few calls from anonymous numbers had come through over the last week or so. She was going to tell Jeremy about them, but now…well, there was no point worrying him any further than he already was. Besides, the calls were probably nothing. No doubt they were just a wrong number.

"I should get going. I need to get to the station." He lifted his hand in a wave and started walking away.

For a moment, she thought about calling him back, but he needed time. He'd come around. Besides, she was already running late.

She glanced at her phone to check the time and smiled when she saw the text from Nick displayed on the screen.

I'm waiting. Let me put a ring on it.

It wasn't real. She knew that. Still, the idea of Nick slipping a ring on her finger sent a crazy kind of thrill through her. Fake or not, she was excited.

———

"It's too big, Nick. No." Char shook her head and backed away from the diamond solitaire ring he held out to her.

It was big. That was the point. He had the money to afford an amazing ring. No one was going to believe it if Charlotte wore some sort of dinky, diamond chip on her finger. She needed a real ring. One that was worthy of her.

They'd been looking at rings for ten minutes and so far hadn't agreed on anything at all. Katie had insisted on watching Amelia for him, so Nick could focus on Charlotte and the task at hand. Despite the fact that they couldn't seem to agree, he was enjoying his time alone with her. Very much.

"That's the point," he insisted. But she still shook her head and backed away. "Char, you deserve this ring. It's gorgeous."

He meant it, too. She absolutely deserved a gorgeous engagement ring, and maybe some earrings and a necklace to go with it. As far as Nick was concerned, she deserved any and all of the jewelry he could give her after what she was doing for him. In fact, it didn't seem like it was enough. Not at all.

She shook her head again and crossed her arms over her chest.

Her stubbornness was so cute, Nick almost laughed. As it was, he smiled and lowered the ring. "Okay," he finally conceded. "That one isn't your style then. You pick one."

"Really?"

He did laugh then. "Of course. This is your ring, Charlotte. I want you to love it."

She looked at him with such a sweet smile that for a minute, Nick could imagine actually giving her the ring for real. It was a ridiculous thought, completely out of left field, considering what they were doing and that they really hardly knew each other at all. But still. *The kiss.*

Okay, *all* the kisses.

Every time they shared a kiss, it was so much better than the one before. *Would it always be that way?* Damn, he hoped so. Because fake engagement or not, kissing Charlotte was one hundred percent real.

"Which one of these rings would you choose for your engagement ring?" Nick handed the solitaire he was still holding back to the owner of the jewelry store and stepped back so Charlotte could have full access to the display case. He watched as she approached and scanned her eyes over the section once, and then twice without picking anything out. "Really, Char. There must be something that catches your eye."

She tilted her head and looked up at him with a sly smile.

"Which one is it?" he prompted.

"You're never going to guess."

Nick was not one to back down from a challenge. Ever. He stepped forward and scanned the rings Char had stopped in front of. "Well, I know it's not that one." He pointed to the five carat solitaire the jeweler had just returned to the display. "And it's the biggest one in here."

"Precisely what I don't like about it."

Nick glanced up at her, and Char raised her eyebrow with a quick wink.

He should have known. Flashy wasn't her style. In fact... with a new idea, he examined the display case.

Something classic, but understated. Nothing too flashy or in your face. Elegant. And... "That one." He tapped the glass in front of an oval-shaped emerald stone surrounded by tiny diamonds on a gold band. "Yes. Definitely. That's the one."

The jeweler smiled and silently moved to pick the ring out of the case. He handed it to Nick, who turned it over in his hand so the light could reflect from it. It was a stunning ring. Completely unpredictable and perfect for Charlotte. Slowly, he turned, the ring between his fingers. "Is this the one you would pick?"

The look on her face told him everything he needed to know.

She nodded quickly, her eyes shiny. "It's beautiful."

He nodded slightly, so she held out her finger and he slipped it on. "It looks amazing."

Charlotte stared, unspeaking, at the ring on her finger. After a moment, she shook her head. "I can't, Nick. It's too much."

He shook his head sharply. He wasn't going to listen to this again. Surely she knew that money was no object, and it was the perfect ring for her. Now that he'd seen it on her hand, there was no other ring that would even come close to being suitable. There were no other choices. Nick turned his back to her and spoke to the jeweler. "We'll take it."

"No." Charlotte was next to him, placing the ring on the counter. "We won't."

"Char..."

"No, Nick. I told you, it's too much and…" A single tear slipped down her cheek, stopping Nick in his tracks.

The ring forgotten, he turned to Charlotte and put his hands on her arms. "What is it? Are you…" He couldn't finish the sentence. If she was having second thoughts about the whole plan, he didn't know what he would do. But he would never force her to continue with anything she didn't want to do. "If you need to—"

"No." She shook her head and forced a smile. "I'm being silly." She moved to wipe her tear, but he beat her to it and let his finger linger on her cheek. "I don't usually cry," she said. "And I really don't know why I am now. It's just…" She took a deep breath and sighed. "You asked me to pick out the ring that I would choose for my engagement ring and then I started thinking that this"—she glanced over his shoulder and whispered into his ear—"isn't real and it made me kind of sad that I might pick out *the* ring and it wouldn't be…well, you know."

He did.

Slowly, he nodded.

She was giving him so much with this favor, Nick wouldn't take that from her. She deserved to have the ring of her dreams, certainly. But not like this. "I get it." And he really did. It also disappointed him more than he expected that he wasn't the man to be giving her that.

In a different time.

"How about we pick out your second favorite ring, then?"

She smiled and nodded. "I'm sorry, Nick. Really. I'm not usually so…sentimental about this kind of thing."

"It's all good. I understand." He took her hand in his and squeezed gently. "What about we go with something you can wear later then? A gift from me."

For the next few minutes they looked at rings, and finally decided on one they were both happy with. A round cut diamond, surrounded by chips of ruby, her mother's birthstone. It was pretty, but not too flashy. Char liked it, Nick thought it was expensive enough to be suitable, and most importantly, it wasn't her dream ring. Because that ring deserved to be on her finger in an entirely different circumstance.

The idea settled deep into his heart.

A maybe.

A *one day*.

Chapter Ten

IT DIDN'T TAKE the three of them long to fall into an easy rhythm in the guest house. It was small, certainly. But they made it work. Charlotte couldn't help but think maybe it was the close proximity to each other all the time that helped the bond between the three of them grow so strongly, so quickly. But even Amelia seemed to enjoy Charlotte's presence, smiling and laughing more every day.

As far as Charlotte and Nick, once they'd made the decision to keep things light, with no expectations, it had opened up a whole new comfort level between them. They kissed easily, as if it were the most natural thing in the world. She knew Damon and Katie had noticed their increased intimacy, too. She'd seen the raised eyebrows and the smiles and shakes of their heads when they were all together, but she didn't care. They were having fun *and* helping the custody case. Surely when Susan did make her visit, she'd notice the closeness, too.

There was no way not to.

In the evening, over glasses of wine, they would cuddle and kiss and fill each other in on their various personal details that a caseworker might ask if and when she ever popped in for her visit, but they still hadn't taken their relationship to the next level. Not that Char didn't want to. She did.

So badly that at times it was hard to focus on anything else, like the matter at hand. Amelia.

"So when do you think it will happen?" Charlotte asked Nick as she returned from the bedroom after laying Amelia down to sleep. It had been just over a week since she'd moved in and they'd started playing house together, and there'd been no sign of the caseworker popping in again.

In fact, as far as Charlotte knew, nothing had happened in the case at all. At least, nothing Nick had told her. Not that he needed to tell her anything, but Charlotte couldn't help but be invested in the outcome. Not that she wouldn't have been anyway, but now, after living with Nick and Amelia and seeing firsthand how amazing he was with her and how much love he had for her, she couldn't imagine the little girl being anywhere else. She *belonged* with her daddy. One hundred percent.

"I have no idea." Nick finished up putting away the plates he'd just finished washing, hung up the dishtowel, and turned around. "Honestly, I thought it would have happened by now. I don't know why. I mean, I know these things take time, but I'm not used to waiting for things."

And just like that, her focus on the matter at hand was broken, and desire flared through her.

"Is that right?" She crossed the room until she stood in front of him. She lowered her eyelids and bit her bottom lip when she got close. "What else aren't you used to waiting for?" She reached up and let her fingers trace the stubble on his chin. He'd started going longer and longer between shaves. It was unexpected from him. And she liked it. It was gruff and sexy.

Char wasn't usually so forward. In fact, in every one of her past relationships, she'd always been a little tentative, or shy even. She couldn't pinpoint where the change in attitude was coming from, but something about Nick brought it out in her, and…maybe it was their situation, and the fact that there was no real pressure on their relationship. Because it wasn't even a real relationship. It was make-believe, with no expectations, and that made it so much easier to put herself out there and go after what she wanted. Even if it was temporary.

Which was exactly why she was more than ready to go after something else she'd been wanting more and more of lately. And that was only natural, right? It had been *so* long since she'd felt anything. So long since the feel of a man's lips on hers had sparked something deep inside. She was beyond overdue to feel sexy and desirable. She craved it.

Needed it.

For too long, Billy had used sex as a weapon. Withholding it or demanding it as the mood struck. But she was past that; she'd worked through it. Put it in her past. And now…she needed more.

She was pretty sure Nick would agree that this was exactly what they both needed.

And he wasn't complaining either, as he put his hands on her hips and held her firmly in his grasp. "Oh, I think you know what I'm not used to waiting for." He tugged her toward him until his lips crushed hers. One hand slipped behind her head and he held her close as his tongue twisted with hers.

Her body liquefied under his attentions the way it always seemed to, and she melted into the kiss, pushing herself closer to him until they were pressed back up against the kitchen counter. It had been a long time since she'd been intimate with a man, and even longer still since she'd enjoyed it.

Instinctively, Charlotte knew she would more than enjoy any kind of physical activity with Nick. If their kisses were anything to go by.

And oh man, they sure were something to go by.

She was more than ready to take this——whatever it was that

they were doing—to the next level. Char groaned and let her mouth slip away, so she could press kisses on his neck. She inhaled the scent of him, fueling her desire as she alternatively sucked and nibbled on his neck, eliciting moans from him that were making it increasingly difficult to not tear his clothes off right there in the kitchen.

But then again, why not?

She pulled away from him.

"I didn't say stop." He grinned.

"Oh, I wasn't about to stop." Char reached for his belt buckle and his eyes widened in surprise.

What did he think was going to happen?

She slipped the leather through the buckle and yanked it free before tugging his zipper down.

Nick's hand stilled hers and held it in place. "Char?"

She looked up at him with heavily lidded eyes. "You said you weren't used to waiting and—"

"That's not what I...shit." He shook his head sharply. "No. That's not what I...I didn't mean that you...that we...dammit."

"Oh." She'd clearly read the situation wrong. Maybe part of keeping things relaxed and without any expectations was keeping things PG. Mortified, she tried to turn away, but he held her fast.

"No, Charlotte." He cupped her cheek with his hand. "That's not what I was trying to say. Not at all. I want this. I want *you.*"

She forced herself to look at him. "Then what is it?"

He squeezed his eyes shut and when he opened them again, she could see he was struggling with something internally.

"Nick? No expectations, remember?" The words tasted sour on her tongue. She hated it because no matter how many times she said that, or reminded herself that what they weren't real, it sure felt real. Just like what she was about to do felt very, very real. Still, she knew he hadn't promised her more, and he'd definitely not promised her *real*. So she swallowed down the sourness and said, "Don't overthink it. This doesn't have to be anything more than what it is."

And what *was* it?

Way too many thoughts slammed through Nick's consciousness all at once.

It was ridiculous, because it hadn't even been a full year ago when he'd regularly hooked up with women for meaningless sex. He'd never thought about what it *could* mean. Or what it *might* mean. It was sex. That was it. No strings. No expectations.

Just like this.

But it wasn't anything like this. Not even close.

Because Charlotte was…

Don't overthink it, she'd said. Dammit. Didn't she know that that's exactly what he did? He overthought. All. The. Time. It was exactly why he'd become so successful in everything he'd done.

Almost.

Her touch on his skin was like fire. More than anything, Nick wanted to tangle his fingers through her hair, pull her tight to him, and kiss away any more thought until they were both naked and sweaty and—

And why not?

Why shouldn't they take things to the next level? They'd already talked about expectations and where his priorities were. Even if it was getting harder and harder to keep it all straight, because when Char kissed him, the line he'd drawn in the sand blurred immediately. Which was why there were about a million reasons he shouldn't go there with her. Not when he was so confused about what he felt.

But there was also one really damn good reason why he should.

Charlotte.

He'd wanted her almost from the moment he'd laid eyes on her. If circumstances had been different—fuck, he hated that saying. Circumstances *weren't* different. They were right here. Right now. In the exact circumstance that they were in.

And what exactly was wrong with that?

His mind was made up before the thoughts had even fully processed.

Nick took her face in his hands and kissed her. Hard.

She groaned against his mouth, and he was completely lost.

Like a switch flipped, his hands were all over her. And hers on his. He lifted his head up long enough to look in her eyes and see nothing but desire and need. No regret. No hesitation.

Perfect.

Their kisses intensified and then there was no going back. Together, they tugged and pulled until clothes were left in a pile by their feet. It was only when Nick's hands slid down Char's bare, soft skin that he paused for a moment. He took a step back so he could see all of her and sucked in a sharp breath. *Damn.* It wasn't even remotely suitable to describe her beauty and how perfect every part of her was.

And how badly he wanted her.

"Everything okay?"

Her voice snapped him out of the trance she'd put him in and a smile crept over his face. "So much better than okay." He moved quickly then, scooping her up and once more taking her mouth in his. He moved toward the bedroom and stopped.

Amelia was in there. And she could sleep through anything, but somehow that felt wrong.

He turned toward the living room and the tiny couch. No.

Nick turned, Charlotte still in his arms, her legs wrapped tight around him, squeezing into him in a way that was making it very hard to think straight.

Out of options, he turned and set her on the kitchen island. Her eyes grew wide in question, but there was no going back. For either of them.

"I know this isn't what you—"

"It's perfect."

She wrapped her hand around the back of his neck and pulled him in. Perfect didn't even begin to describe what was happening. Not. Even. Close.

"You are so gorgeous, Char."

Nick couldn't help but feel bad for the lack of worshiping of her body he was doing. Because it was so worthy of all the worship. But having his hands on her body and his mouth on hers was making it hard to focus on anything else.

He ran his hands down her curves, cupping her breasts before bending to kiss each of them in turn. Beneath his attentions, she shuddered and moaned.

Charlotte slid her own hands down his body to find the throbbing between his legs. When she took his length in her hand and squeezed, he was done. "Oh," he moaned, dropping his face to nuzzle in her neck. "Careful or you'll—"

"I'll what?" Her tone teased and played.

But he wasn't playing. Not anymore. The intensity with which he needed her was all-encompassing.

"Char...I...oh God..."

Nick lifted his head and took her mouth in his, kissing her hard. She responded by shifting back on the counter, pulling him between her legs, tighter.

He needed a condom. He needed to slow it down. He needed...

"It's okay," she murmured. "I'm on the Pill."

Nick swallowed hard.

And when Char spoke again, there was no more holding back. "I need you, Nick." She tugged him forward. "Now."

There was no way he could argue with that.

He took her breath away when he entered her. She was ready. More than ready, but it had been awhile and the sensation of having him inside her, filling her was beyond intense. Charlotte squeezed her eyes shut with a groan and let her head fall back as he stilled, letting her body adjust to him. But only for a moment before he started to move inside her.

Charlotte gripped his shoulders tight. No doubt her nails dug into his skin, but he didn't seem to mind as he increased his pace.

She lifted her head up to see him, and the sight of him took her breath away again. This time it was because of the way he was looking at her. As if she were the sexiest, most desirable person in the entire world. He was completely lost in her.

A fact that was only confirmed a moment later when he said, "Fuck, Char, you feel absolutely amazing." His words came out on a groan and it was the hottest thing she'd ever heard.

She needed him closer, to feel his body pressed to hers. She shifted up on the counter so she sat up, right on the edge. Nick wrapped his arms tight around her back, holding her against his chest, and she wrapped her legs around his back, holding him tight.

The increased skin contact only heightened every sensation that tore through her, intensifying every thrust. It didn't take long for Char to feel the building tension deep inside her core. She wasn't going to be able to hold back. It was taking everything she had in her not to lose the tenuous grip on her control.

"Let go, Char," Nick murmured. "Let go for me."

She bit down on her bottom lip and squeezed her eyes shut. She wasn't going to be able to hold it off much longer. Her legs started to quake and tremble, and Nick increased his pace of relentless thrusting, driving into her. Just when she was about to scream out her release, he closed his mouth over hers and kissed her hard, swallowing her screams of pleasure with his kiss and giving her the space to experience her climax in full, without fear of waking the baby.

Still kissing, Nick's own release followed moments later. He held her tight. His mouth was still on hers, as they both returned to earth. Their kisses came slower and lazier, until finally, they pulled their mouths away from each other. Nick's lips were turned up in a satisfied smile that she knew must match her own.

He didn't pull away or move to unwrap himself from her, and she, too, stayed wrapped tight around him, selfishly wanting to soak up as much of the moment as she possibly could.

"That was…" He started pressing kisses to her neck and collarbone.

His attentions stirred up a renewed desire, but there was no way. She was exhausted. It was too much. He'd need a rest, too.

"It was," she agreed. "I didn't think it was…mmm." Her words dissolved into groans as he sucked and nibbled on the sensitive skin on her neck. "Nick, I…"

"You want me to stop?"

She shook her head and he chuckled. "Didn't think so."

"But, you…we just…"

"Let me worry about that." He grinned, and it was both the sexiest and sweetest thing she'd ever seen. "But I do think…wait here."

He unwound himself from her body, and Charlotte immediately felt the loss of him. She watched and admired exactly how incredibly sexy he was as he moved through the small guest house. He disappeared into the bedroom and returned with blankets, pillows, and quilts that he arranged on the floor in front of the couch after moving the coffee table aside.

When he was done making up what could only be described as a nest, he returned to her still on the kitchen island and kissed her, his hand on her chin, holding her to him. Char couldn't help it: every time they kissed, it melted her a little. It was a good thing she was sitting down, because she was positive her legs were completely incapable of supporting her. She gasped a little as he once again scooped her up and this time carried her to the bed he'd made for them on the floor.

"This is sweet," she said after Nick deposited her on the blankets.

He looked down at her and moved like a cat until he was overtop her, with a wicked grin on his face that sent a shock of desire once more between her legs.

"I assure you, sweetheart, there is nothing sweet about my intentions." His eyes flared before lowering his mouth to hers once again.

It wasn't until later—much later—when Nick's arm was draped over her waist and he was pressed up tightly against her, his deep breathing telling her he'd finally exhausted himself enough to sleep, that Char let herself think that maybe, even for a moment, whatever it was that was happening between them just might be more than either of them were letting themselves believe.

Chapter Eleven

THE PAINT COLOR WAS PERFECT. Char swiped the brush across the blank wall again and stepped back with a satisfied grin. The cabins were comprised almost entirely of logs, but there were a few interior walls that Travis had put up in some of the bigger cabins to section off the bathrooms and bedrooms. She'd tried at least five colors, but none of them looked quite right. Until now.

"Perfect." She couldn't help but laugh at herself when she realized she still had two coats to do. The one swipe from her brush wasn't even close to being done. Not that she minded. For the last week, she'd immersed herself in the design and planning of the Lynx Creek cabins, and she was loving every single minute of it.

It felt good to be doing what she loved again. Really good. And most importantly, Steph was happy with the early results, too.

She'd set up each cabin to be a little bit different than the last, each with their own theme to keep them unique but at the same time cozy and comfortable. But this cabin, the one tucked up farthest in the hills, was going to be her favorite. Because of its location, completely secluded and surrounded by tall pines, it was obviously going to be the *Lumberjack* cabin. She'd picked out a red and black plaid bedspread and had found various *lumberjack* paraphernalia to adorn the walls and the couch—when the furniture was finally delivered in the coming weeks. Including a really nice antique ax that would look fantastic on the wall by the door.

Char put down her paintbrush and picked up the ax, giving it a little swing. The ring on her left hand caught the sun as she lowered the tool safely back to the ground and once again, like so many other times since Nick had put it on her finger, just over a week ago, she stopped and stared at it.

It was a gorgeous ring, even if it wasn't *the* ring and it had been given to her in the most messed-up situation. Still, she couldn't help but think that maybe, under different circumstances, or even when all of this mess was sorted out... maybe...the situation wouldn't be quite so messed up and the ring might actually represent more than a solution to keep Amelia safe and with her father. Maybe it could be more?

It wasn't the first time Charlotte had let herself think that way. And it concerned her that it might not even be the last. But she couldn't help it.

She hadn't meant for it to happen, and she'd meant it when she'd said that she didn't want anything serious, but still... playing house with Nick and Amelia was starting to feel more and more real as the days went on. Waking up to the smell of fresh coffee brewing and the happy sounds of a little girl who had very quickly worked her way into Charlotte's heart, followed by a good morning kiss from Nick, had become a pretty amazing way to start her days.

But not as amazing as how she'd been ending her days. Wrapped in the arms of a strong, sexy, and smart man who challenged her mind with no end of ideas about her business and never seemed to tire of hearing about her latest design finds or what she was working on at the cabins before their conversations would inevitably dissolve into kisses and touches that made her body come alive over and over again.

Yes. It was a pretty easy life to get used to.

She took a breath and pulled her gaze away from her ring as her cell phone rang. Without glancing at the caller ID, she snatched it up.

"Hello?" She practically singsonged into the phone.

"Damn."

Charlotte's heart stopped for a split second.

"It's good to hear that voice. Baby, where've you been?"

She punched the button to end the call and dropped the phone on the floor in front of her, staring at it as if it would explode at any second.

No.

Billy.

The anonymous calls with no one on the other end. They weren't wrong numbers. But...

Billy didn't know how to find her.

Not that it would take a genius to know she was back in Glacier Falls. But no one had her number. Only her close friends and family. And there's no way he'd come for her. He wasn't that kind of guy. He was a controlling, emotionally abusive asshole, but he was also a total coward. There's no way he'd set foot in Glacier Falls. Not when he knew her brother would make sure it was the last time he ever used that foot.

She'd been so sure he'd leave her alone. He'd go off and lick his wounds and move onto someone else.

She'd been so *sure*.

Which was why she'd never said anything about the other calls.

She was such an idiot.

The phone rang again, and she fell to the floor and put her arms over her head. She couldn't do this. She couldn't let this man come in and ruin what was going so well. He'd already taken so much from her. She couldn't deal with it. She couldn't —*no!*

What she couldn't do was sit there and let herself be a victim again. The words of her therapist, Lauren, ran through her head. "You are strong and capable. You always were. He didn't take that from you; he just made you forget for a little bit. It's time to remember who you are."

Remember who you are.

Char took a deep breath and picked up the still ringing phone. She stared at it for a moment before closing her eyes and pushing the button to answer it. "You need to leave me alone, Billy."

"I miss you."

"No." She worked hard to keep her voice even and strong.

"I do. You left me."

She nodded, but didn't speak.

"You weren't supposed to leave, Char. That wasn't part of the plan."

"It was part of mine." *Right. Strong.* "We're done, Billy. You need to move on."

"You shouldn't have left."

Was that a threat?

He'd never been violent with her. Not really. Well, not more than once or twice. At the time, she hadn't considered his rough handling of her abuse. But it was. She knew that now.

"Good-bye, Billy." She exhaled slowly, letting the tension fall from her shoulders. She was about to hang up when his words caught her attention.

"It'll never be good-bye, Char. Never."

She sucked in a breath and ended the call. She didn't want to admit it, but he'd gotten to her. He'd—

"Who was on the phone?"

Nick stepped into the *Lumberjack* cabin, hoping to surprise Char with lunch, but he wasn't prepared to find her sitting on the floor. And he definitely wasn't prepared to see her looking so shaken.

"Who was on the phone?"

He hadn't caught much of the conversation, but he was pretty sure he'd heard the name Billy. And if he'd heard what he thought he'd heard, he wasn't happy about it.

Char's head jerked up and he could see without her even saying anything that he was right.

"Dammit." Nick fell to his knees on the floor in front of her. "It was Billy?" He pulled her into his arms and muttered under his breath, "Fuck." A protective surge toward Charlotte washed over him. And why wouldn't it? They were…friends. *Good* friends. He'd protect any of his friends the same way. Just because it was Charlotte didn't mean anything.

"It's fine. It's—"

"Not fine. I'll destroy him, Char. I—"

"You won't and you know it."

He pulled her tighter to him and stroked her silky hair. "I won't. You're right. But I swear, if he touches one hair on your head, I'll—"

"He won't." She pulled back and looked him in the eye. "He's not going to bother me. He's just full of hot air and he's feeling like a wounded little boy, that's all. He's harmless."

Nick wasn't so sure, but arguing with her about a situation he knew very little about wasn't going to be productive. Instead, he sat flat on his ass, and spread his legs wide so he could pull her into him and wrap his arms around her. She relaxed into his arms and he could feel some of the tension escape her body as he held her.

He'd meant what he said, even if it had come out a little

harsher than he'd intended it to. If that waste of space, excuse of a man tried to hurt Charlotte in any way, he would destroy him without even hesitating. No, he wouldn't hurt him. He was too smart for that. But Nick had the means to make his life as unpleasant as possible. If he messed with Charlotte, he was messing with Nick. And if that was the case, that loser didn't know what he was getting himself into. And he certainly wasn't going to like it.

Nick forced himself to slow his breathing and he kissed the top of Char's head. And then, because when it came to this woman, he simply couldn't seem to keep his hands or his lips off her, he moved his kiss lower, to the sensitive skin behind her ear that always made her squirm when he kissed her there.

Sure enough, she wiggled her way back into him, pressing her peach-perfect ass against his growing desire and tipped her head back so it rested on his shoulder, and he could have easier access. But Nick wanted more than kisses on the neck. So much more. This woman made him want things that he had no business wanting. But he couldn't help it. And anyway, he wasn't sure he wanted to.

He wrapped an arm around her and spun Char on the wood floor so she was facing him and he could gently lay her back onto the floor where he could kiss her properly. There was still no furniture in the cabin, but that wouldn't stop him. It might even be extra fun.

The more of Charlotte that he experienced, the more he wanted. She was like a drug. Even though whatever was happening between them was meant to be an arrangement, it was starting to feel like a whole lot more than that, and very quickly. Maybe he should be worried about how close they were getting, but he wasn't. Not even a little.

Nick lowered his body, so his mouth could close over hers, but moments before his lips found their target, she wiggled underneath him and slipped out from under him.

"I'm working," she protested with a smile. "I have so much to do here and—I didn't even ask...is everything okay? You don't usually pop in unannounced." She asked the question as she got to her feet and picked up a paintbrush.

She looked over to him as Nick flipped around so he was sitting and could watch her bend to dip the paint in the bucket. If he couldn't kiss her, a close second would have to be watching her bend over. He wiggled his eyebrows and she laughed.

"I just wanted to see you." It was the truth. He'd been running a few errands and when he popped into the Hub, Katie's adventure equipment store, she'd practically stolen Amelia right out of his arms and told him to take a *Dad break*. So he'd done just that. But faced with an hour or two without the baby, the only person he'd wanted to spend that time with was Charlotte. No contest. "And I brought snacks." He got to his feet and fetched the coffee and bag of muffins he'd picked up at Sweetie Pies before coming. He'd ditched them at the front when he'd seen Char on the floor when he'd come in.

"I like snacks."

He laughed. "I brought bubbly, too." He held up the bottle of Prosecco he'd picked up last minute. "We never really toasted to your new job and now that you're almost done..."

"That sounds awesome." She winked over her shoulder and turned back to the wall she was painting. "Just let me finish this—" She squealed when Nick wrapped his arms around her and put a cheeky kiss on her neck. "Nick!" Charlotte spun around and swiped his cheek with the paintbrush.

He jumped back and his mouth dropped open. "You did not just do that?"

She wiggled her hips and grinned at him. "Oh, I think I just did."

Nick curled his lips up in a wicked smile of his own. "It's on, baby." He moved quickly, grabbing the extra paintbrush and dipping it in the paint before she would have a chance to realize what was happening.

"Oh no." Charlotte laughed. "Nick!"

Her protests fueled him as he returned the favor and dotted paint on her nose before she once again jabbed her brush in his direction.

"I don't think so." Nick used his longer legs and arms to his advantage and moved quickly to wrap her up in his arms, pinning hers down by her sides so he could not only prevent further attacks, but also take the opportunity to kiss her. Just as she always did, Charlotte melted against his lips and deepened the kiss with a small moan.

He'd kissed his share of women in his life, but never had it felt like it did with Charlotte. Perfect and totally meant to be.

Painting forgotten, Nick pressed Char up against the wall and slid one hand down her body, to the button on her jeans. It was becoming a problem, his total inability to keep his hands off her. But as far as problems went, it seemed like a good one to have.

"Nick…"

"Yes?" He kissed her neck and any protest she was about to make dissolved on her lips.

"Knock knock!" A sharp rap on the open cabin door startled Nick into jumping backward. "Oh, I didn't mean to interrupt anything."

Charlotte's face bloomed hot and red in an instant. She glared at Nick, who although still standing close, was far enough away that at least they could pull off some semblance of decency despite the fact that what they were about to do before being interrupted was anything but decent. Especially considering it was Susan Johnson, the caseworker—and the one person who had the power to make life-changing decisions for them—who'd done the interrupting.

"Hi, Susan." Nick flashed her a genuine smile, easily pulling himself together as if nothing had just happened. He offered her his hand, but quickly pulled it back when he realized the paintbrush was still in it.

To her credit, Susan took it all in stride. She shook her head and smiled. "I really am sorry to interrupt," she said. "But it's nice to see that your affection hasn't been affected by having a baby around." As if she'd just remembered the reason for her visit, she glanced around the tiny cabin. "Where is Amelia?"

"She's with friends in town," Nick said. "Katie and Damon Banks. They insisted I come surprise Charlotte with a break from her work."

Susan raised her eyebrows, and still standing in the corner, Charlotte wanted to completely self-combust from embarrassment.

"I brought her coffee and muffins," Nick said, as if that explained what they'd been doing.

"Ah, yes." Susan nodded. "That's how I found you up here, actually."

Charlotte put her paintbrush down, and adjusted her clothing as best she could while Susan spoke.

"I went up to your house," Susan continued. "At ElkView. Beautiful property."

"It really is," Charlotte agreed, finally able to speak.

"But when I didn't find you, I thought I might go down to that amazing bakery we met at the other day and get a little treat while I waited. Of course, a small-town coffee shop is the perfect place to collect information as well."

Charlotte forced the smile to stay on her face despite the fear that ran through her. *Had she heard any gossip about them?* Surely no one would be stupid enough to say anything.

"Is that right?" Nick must have been freaking out as well, but to his credit, he kept his cool. "And what did you learn?"

"Well," Susan said. "I learned that these cabins here are Stephanie Starz's newest project and that you're working on the designs." She looked to Charlotte, who nodded her confirmation. "I also learned that you'd just been in, Nick, and were headed up here to see Charlotte, so I took a chance on catching you both up here. Oh, and..." Susan blushed. "And maybe Stephanie Starz is here, too?"

Charlotte shook her head. "Sorry. She's actually in the city right now."

"Oh, that's fine." Susan tried not to show her disappointment, and Char tried not to smile at just how star-struck the woman was and instead, changed the subject.

"I'm sorry we weren't home today. Will you have to come back, or—"

"Well, it is quite a drive out here..." Susan sucked in a breath. "I hate to cut your dad break short," she said to Nick. "But would it be okay if—"

"That sounds good." He cut her off before she could finish. "I can go pick up Amelia and meet you both up at the house if that works?"

Of course it worked. The whole point of...well, everything, was to convince this woman that they were a loving couple and the best possible choice for Amelia. Which meant, as long as it worked for Susan, it worked for her. The painting could wait.

And so could the kissing.

It was hours later by the time they finished up with Susan and Charlotte was able to get back to her painting and even later when she was able to get back to the kissing and cuddling. It had been a long day but a good one, and she was very quickly getting used to finishing a long day in Nick's arms.

"That went well today, don't you think?" She was tucked into the crook of his arm, cuddled with her head on his chest.

"It really did. Thank you for leaving the cabins this afternoon. I know you have so much work to do and—"

"Hey." She turned a little so she could look up at him. "That's what this is all about, isn't it?" She felt a pang in her chest even as she spoke the words. It was very quickly becoming *not* what it was all about. Of course, Amelia was the number-one concern, obviously. But every day that passed, she couldn't help that her feelings were growing for both of them. It was getting harder and harder to remember that it was all supposed to be temporary, and they'd agreed to easy, with no feelings. It was getting *really* hard.

Nick hesitated and stroked her hair off her face. "It is," he finally agreed. "And I do think it went really well today. We answered all her questions, and Amelia was extra smiley and happy today."

"She was," Char agreed. "And do you think it helped when she walked in on us earlier? Like…maybe it gave her the feeling that we were a real couple with real feelings?"

He stiffened under her.

Did she go too far? Did he think she was searching or digging for more?

Dammit.

The last thing she wanted was for Nick to think that she was going back on her promise to keep things light and easy, with no expectations. She didn't want to spook him now. Especially when things were so critical. Susan said she was going to put her recommendation in right away and then the whole case would have to go to the courts. Of course, Char didn't hear all the details because Nick had asked her to put Amelia down for her nap while they finished up. Not that she minded, but she couldn't help but feel like she missed some details about the case and what was going on.

"Char, about—"

"I thought we nailed it." She interrupted him and put a bright smile on her face before he could say anything that might end their fake relationship prematurely—or worse, do anything to hurt Amelia's chance of staying with her father. "And don't worry about me," she continued. "I'll keep doing my part and playing the role of devoted and madly in love fiancée." She pushed up enough to give him a quick kiss and then flipped over to turn off the bedside light. "I'm exhausted. Good night."

She *was* exhausted. But it wasn't playing the role of devoted and madly in love fiancée that was hard work; it was pretending that it wasn't exactly how she felt that was taking its toll on her.

Chapter Twelve

"SHE REALLY IS the sweetest little girl in the world, isn't she?" Hope Langdon tickled under Amelia's chin until she giggled and squealed in delight, causing Hope to laugh, too. "So interactive. I can't wait until Cole gets to that stage, too. Not that I'm rushing it," she added quickly as she glanced over at her own baby with loving eyes. The little boy was fast asleep in his Auntie Faith's arms. "I'll keep him tiny as long as I can." At only a few months old, Cole was still pretty small, and a perfectly sweet baby. "But I could do with some more sleep at night, you know what I mean?"

Charlotte smiled in understanding, despite the fact that she had no frame of reference about how a baby slept at night. Amelia was an excellent sleeper, and as far as Char was concerned, was the best baby in the world. It hadn't taken her long to completely and totally fall in love with the little girl. Not that it was hard; Amelia captivated everyone with her bright-blue eyes and sweet smile.

When Hope had called to invite her over for tea and a little girl time, Charlotte had jumped at the chance. She'd known the twins in school when they were kids, but Char was older than them, so they didn't really hang out at all. Still, growing up in a small town, everyone kind of knew everyone. And a baby playdate sounded like a fantastic opportunity for them to reconnect.

Katie had come, too, and she'd brought along Natalie Collins, who was one of the firefighters who worked with her brother at the station and was new to town.

"I wish I could tell you our secret," Char said with an apologetic shrug. "But I can't take any credit for how well she sleeps. Nick said she's always been…" It wasn't a secret to any of them that she and Nick were faking their engagement; still, it felt strange to talk about it. Especially because more and more, whatever was happening between her and Nick was starting to feel very real.

"What is going on there?" Faith asked the question with a tilt of her head and wink in Katie's direction.

Char spun around and glared at Katie. *What had she said?*

"Don't get mad at Katie," Faith said, picking up on what Charlotte was thinking. "All she said was that the two of you look really cute together."

"That's not all she said." It was Natalie who chimed in with a wiggle of her eyebrows.

Hope laughed, causing Amelia to join in, too.

Charlotte took her time looking around the circle of women in turn. Finally, she swallowed hard. "You all know that we're only pretending to be together for the caseworker, right?" She focused on Katie as she spoke, but her friend said nothing in return, only winked.

"Faith?" She turned to the blonde-haired beauty. "You know that, right? I mean, Nick and I are just…" There was no easy way to finish that sentence. Not one that made sense, anyway.

"You're what?"

Char spun around to look at Katie, who'd asked the question.

"We're doing this for Amelia." Charlotte could feel herself growing frustrated. How was she supposed to explain to her friends what was going on between her and Nick in a way that they would understand? Especially when she herself didn't understand it. "We need it to be believable," she explained. "It's important that Amelia can stay with Nick. We had a really good visit with the caseworker the other day. She surprised us at the cabins and...well, it all ended up really positive. I think she'll put in a good recommendation, which is important because the courts don't often rule in favor of a single father and...well, they do. But it's harder and having a stable home situation makes it more—"

"And you two are stable?" It was Natalie who asked. "I mean, if the engagement is fake, is it really stable for the baby to be—"

"She belongs with her father." Char cut her off and forced herself to swallow hard. She was almost positive that Natalie's opinion of what was happening was at least partly swayed by her brother. After all, Jeremy had made no secret of how he didn't approve of Charlotte and Nick's arrangement. No doubt he'd let that opinion be heard at the fire hall, too.

"I don't doubt that, Charlotte," Natalie said. "And honestly, I didn't mean to imply anything else. I'm sorry if it...well...I can't imagine the stress Nick's under, trying to make all this happen and—"

"Where does she get her eye color?" Faith interrupted the conversation, completely oblivious to what was happening. "They're so blue. Nick's eyes are dark, aren't they?"

Charlotte let the conversation with Natalie slide away, which was probably for the best, and looked at Faith, who was staring at Amelia.

"And this hair." Faith patted Amelia's blonde, slightly red-tinged hair that had been coming in thicker and thicker lately. "Nick's coloring is so dark. Her mother must be really fair, and with some very strong genetics."

Faith laughed, but Char didn't join in. Just because she knew the truth about Amelia's parentage didn't mean that everyone needed to know. She didn't want to do anything that would risk the custody case.

It was true that Amelia didn't resemble Nick at all. "I don't know anything about her mother," Char said. "But obviously Amelia takes after her."

"Well, you know, I can't see even a bit of me in Cole," Hope said. "He's a carbon copy of his father." She laughed. "It's so strange the way genetics work, isn't it?"

The women all laughed.

"I hope our baby is the perfect mixture of Damon and—"

"What?" It was Faith who cut her off. Her mouth hung open. "*Your* baby? Are you...did you..."

"Are you pregnant?" Hope helped her sister out. "Katie? Really?"

Katie nodded and the group erupted in squeals. "We're not really telling people yet," Katie said when the excitement died down. "It's super-new still and we agreed we wouldn't tell people yet, but...my secret's safe with you all, right?"

Of course it was, and they all swore their silence.

It wasn't until Katie and Char were on their way home that Charlotte asked her friend, "Why is it that you didn't want to say anything about being pregnant? It's so exciting."

"It is," Katie agreed. "But a lot of women don't say anything about being pregnant until after the first trimester."

Char had heard that, but she'd never really understood why. She told Katie as much.

"Because what if it doesn't work out?"

"That would be terrible," Charlotte agreed. "No matter what, it would be terrible. But if your friends and family knew, then at least you'd have them to help you through it instead of going through it alone."

Katie thought about that for a moment and finally nodded. "I guess that's true," she said after a minute. "But can I ask you a question then?"

Of course Charlotte agreed.

"So why is it that you aren't telling anyone about you and Nick?"

Behind the wheel of the car, Charlotte tensed.

"I mean, I get it…it might not work out. But what if it does? Either way, don't you want your friends and family to know?"

Charlotte swallowed hard. "There's nothing going on with me and Nick. We're doing this for—"

"I know why you're doing it." Katie cut her off. "But I also know I'm not blind. And don't forget, you're talking to the queen of *fake relationships*." She used air quotes. "I know what I see."

Charlotte navigated the car through the gates at ElkView and up the hill toward the guest house.

"And you two are definitely more than pretending. It's okay to—"

"Oh, look." Charlotte interrupted her friend. "We have visitors." There was a red, older model sedan parked next to the guest house. Nick had left for the city for the day, with the plan to stay the night if his meetings ran long, but he hadn't said anything about a visitor and the caseworker had already been there. Whomever it was, Char didn't have a good feeling about it.

"Were you expecting guests?"

Charlotte shook her head and tried to rack her brain for who it might be. Surely, it wasn't Billy. But it might be…he'd called at least four more times since the first time at the cabin. Every time, she'd hung up on him. But the last time, before she could end the call, she could have sworn she'd heard him say something about coming to see her. At the time, she'd been sure he was just blowing smoke. She hadn't even mentioned it to Nick. After all, he had enough to worry about. And she'd meant it when she'd said that Billy wasn't man enough to actually confront her. *But...what if she'd been wrong?*

She couldn't take the baby into that situation; it wasn't safe. "Who do you think it is?"

For a moment, she considered telling Katie the truth about Billy, but immediately dismissed it. She didn't need anyone worrying about something that likely wasn't even a thing. In fact, she was sure she was overreacting. *But still...*

She swallowed hard and forced a smile to her face. "Would you mind taking Amelia back to your place for a bit? I just want to make sure it's not a salesperson or something."

Katie gave her a look, but nodded the way Charlotte hoped she would. "Of course. I love spending time with her."

Char quickly unbuckled the baby and handed her to Katie, who immediately started cooing and making the baby giggle. She waited until they'd disappeared down the path toward the main house and then she straightened her shoulders, took a deep breath, and went around to the front of the house.

"So what exactly is it that you're saying?" Nick paced across the office and back toward his lawyer, Chris. Some meetings were too important to have over the phone, which was why when Chris called to say he had news, Nick made the trip to the city to have the conversation in person. Besides that, he didn't want to worry Charlotte with any of this. There was no point in both of them being stressed out or completely preoccupied with the *what-ifs*. So he'd gone to the city to try to sort it out before it went any further and he needed to get her involved. He'd fix it. "She's going to fight me for custody?"

"I didn't say that." Chris crossed his leg over his knee and sat back in his chair behind the massive mahogany desk, looking far too comfortable for Nick's liking.

He needed the man to be even a fraction as worked up as he was. Because this could not happen.

"I said that she's reached out to us."

"With a lawyer?"

"No."

Nick exhaled the breath he'd been holding. No lawyer meant she couldn't possibly be serious about coming after Amelia. There was nothing to worry about.

"She doesn't need a lawyer, Nick."

"What?" Nick spun around on his heel. "You always need a lawyer for these things. We'll squash her in court."

Chris sighed and sat up. "*If* it gets to court."

"Of course it will get to court." His blood pressure was rising. Chris, who'd always been just as much of a friend as a top-notch lawyer, was *really* starting to piss him off. "Why wouldn't it go to court? She's a druggie who gave away her baby." Nick struggled to control his voice. "Jessica abandoned her, Chris. No judge in the world will take her away from her father and—"

"You're not her father, Nick."

"Fuck!" He slammed his fist on the desk, the battle for control lost. To his credit, Chris didn't flinch.

Nick put both his hands flat on the smooth wood of the desk and dropped his head. He worked hard to drag in one breath after another until he no longer saw red in his vision. Or at least, less red. "She is my daughter." He spoke each word through gritted teeth when he looked up. "It's your job to make sure that doesn't change."

Chris nodded curtly. "I'm doing everything I can, Nick.

You know that. But these cases…they aren't black and white. And if the judge sees that Jessica is trying to improve her life in order to regain custody, well…I'm afraid there won't be—"

"Don't say it."

His lawyer closed his lips tightly together and shook his head.

"I mean it, Chris." Nick slowly stood and rolled his shoulders back. "We can't let that happen. She *left* her baby. *Left her.* There can't be any coming back from that." But even as he spoke the words, he knew there was. The system was set up to give second chances, or third, or…whatever it took to keep families together. Sometimes it worked. Other times it failed miserably.

He'd been a victim of that failure. He would have been unequivocally better off if his mother hadn't been given *any* chances after she'd shown herself to be unfit. It didn't matter how many times she told the caseworkers that she'd been to rehab, that she was clean, that she had a job, that she was devoted to her son.

It was all a lie.

He wouldn't let that happen to Amelia. She deserved so much better.

He paced to the picture window and pressed one hand against the floor-to-ceiling glass as he stared out over the city skyline and thought about his options. What few there were. Finally, he dropped his head in defeat and turned back to Chris, who was waiting patiently. "Tell me what to do."

Chris sat up and rolled his chair toward his desk. "We play nice," he said simply. "Jessica will be contacting you. She wants to see Amelia."

Nick bristled at the thought.

"The best thing to do is allow her to see the baby. Hopefully she'll be happy with just a visit."

"What do you mean, *just?*"

"You don't want to hear this, but if she wants to take the baby overnight—"

"No."

Chris sighed. "You're not her biological father, Nick."

"She doesn't know that."

"Doesn't she?"

He didn't know. He assumed she knew, but his investigation had shown she'd gone through a really wild phase; she might have lost track of the timeline and really think that Nick was the father. Or, and it was more likely, she might have just thought he was the best financially to take care of the baby. "I don't know."

"Well, if she does…" Chris shook his head. "Let's just hope it doesn't come to that, because you don't have any legal right to withhold the child if that's the case."

"That's fucking crazy. She's a baby. Who's looking after her rights?" Nick could feel his blood pressure rising again.

"I get it," Chris said. "I really do."

Nick bit his tongue and let Chris continue.

"I know it's not what you want to hear," he said. "But the judge will pay attention to your behavior, and judges like to see everyone playing nicely in the sandbox. It will work in your favor. In the meantime, you tell me that you have yourself a fiancée?" He raised his eyebrows.

Despite the tense situation, he smiled the way he always did when he thought about Charlotte. "I do."

Chris shook his head. "I don't think I should even ask about how that came about, but I'm glad. As long as she's a solid woman, that will work in your favor, too."

Nick moved to the couch across the room and sank into it. "She's a solid woman. Doesn't do drugs. Only drinks socially. She's never been arrested and she has a solid career that's just starting to really take off. She's great. And she's so amazing with Amelia, too. She really cares about her." She was great.

And in so many other ways that Nick was not about to start explaining to Chris. Let alone the way they'd very quickly taken their relationship to the next level and how it all felt so natural just to be with her that Nick spent most of his time reminding himself that they'd promised each other easy, with no expectations. Just when he was thinking that there might actually be more to what was going on between them, Char had reminded him quite clearly the other night that there wasn't.

He took a breath. "She's really, really great."

"That's all really...*great*," Chris said with an odd look. "But if she's that involved with Amelia, you should probably prepare her for what it will mean if Jessica shows up."

No. He wouldn't do that because it wouldn't get to that point. He'd told Charlotte how terrible it was to be raised by an addict, and Jessica was...*no.* He wasn't going to let it happen, so there was no point in worrying her about it when there wasn't going to be anything to worry about.

"She should be on the same page." Chris looked at him and dropped his pen on the desk. "But don't panic yet, okay?"

That was easy for him to say.

"Just wait and see what happens. If Jessica does contact you, we'll make sure she has a clean drug test and a recommendation from her caseworker, okay? We won't just let her take the baby. We'll keep her safe, Nick."

Nick stood and rolled his neck before staring directly at his lawyer. "Damn straight we will."

Charlotte took a moment to practice the cleansing breaths her therapist had taught her when it came to dealing with or thinking about Billy. Of course, that had been in regards to dealing with memories of him, or the occasional phone call.

That had not included how she should handle things when it came to dealing with him in person.

Still. She'd come a long way. She wasn't the same woman who'd fallen for his bullshit before. She was different. Confident. Sure of herself. Strong. He couldn't get to her. He couldn't hurt her.

She exhaled and rounded the corner, ready to see the man who'd tried to take everything from her.

It wasn't Billy waiting for her, but a woman. She stood to the far edge of the patio, her back to Charlotte, gazing out over the valley below, and she didn't appear to have noticed Charlotte yet.

Char moved so the table was between her and the stranger before she spoke. "Hello? Can I help you?"

Jolted from whatever trance she'd been in, the woman turned around. "It sure is beautiful here," she said, without acknowledging Char at all. "Peaceful. Like you could really get lost in yourself, you know?"

Char nodded despite the fact that she had no idea what the other woman was talking about. "Can I help you?" She shaded her eyes in order to see the woman a little better. "Were you looking for someone?"

Finally, the woman took a step close enough that Charlotte could see her a little better. She was pretty. With blonde, wavy hair that fell over her slight shoulders. She was dressed simply in jeans and a sweater that was probably a bit too warm for the late April day. She wore sunglasses, so Char couldn't see her eyes, but something about the woman gave off the air of exhaustion. As if she hadn't gotten enough sleep the night before. Or the night before that.

"I'm looking for Nick," she said after a moment. "Nick Newton."

Char nodded but didn't speak. She tried to keep her breathing even, but something about the woman set off alarm bells, and she sure as hell hoped it wasn't who she thought it could be. But surely she was wrong. Nick said she was out of the picture. Not a concern. But…maybe this woman was an old girlfriend trying to track him down? *Yes. That must be*—

"I knew he'd have a nice house, but this is…" The woman turned and once again stared out over the valley. "It's amazing."

Char worked hard to keep her breathing under control. Because, no, this was not any ordinary woman from Nick's past. On some level, she knew it the moment she'd seen her. This petite blonde woman was Amelia's mother. Charlotte knew it in her gut, and it was a million times worse than if it had been Billy waiting for her.

She tried to keep her voice light when she asked the question that would confirm what she already knew. "And you are?"

The woman turned then and slipped her glasses off her face so Char was looking directly into eyes that were identical to baby Amelia's, when she spoke with complete confidence. "My name is Jessica Silva. I'm here for my daughter."

Chapter Thirteen

"WHAT THE ACTUAL..." Stephanie collapsed against the railing, unable to speak between gasping breaths. She dropped her head down in an effort to catch her breath. When Nick had called to tell her he was in town for a quick trip, she'd jumped at the chance to see him, of course. He was one of her best friends and with their crazy schedules, she'd take whatever opportunity she could to catch up with him. But she had not thought that his idea of catching up would be on a running track, sprinting until her lungs were on fire.

"Trouble keeping up?" Nick looked at her with complete seriousness.

"Yes," she said as she stood straight again. "Of course I'm having trouble keeping up. What the hell has gotten into you? Besides, I thought you were busy working on your dad bod now. How are you even so fit?"

That got a smirk out of him, but only a quick one. "Ready to go again?"

"Nick!"

He looked at her with genuine surprise.

"Talk to me. What has you all fired up like a crazy man?"

Nick bounced on the balls of his feet. "I met with my lawyer earlier." He shook his head before she could ask for more details. "No. I'm not talking about it."

Steph understood, as much as anyone could understand. She also knew if he wanted advice, he'd ask for it. And he hadn't.

"You okay?"

He nodded but then shrugged.

"Mostly okay?"

That got a small smile out of her friend. "I am. Thank you. I know you're just concerned and I appreciate it, but there's just nothing more we can do. We're really doing all we can. The other day, we had our caseworker visit and I think she... well, I..." His mouth widened into a full-fledged smile.

"We?" Steph wiggled her eyebrow. "We as in, Char and Nick?"

"Well, yes...we are doing this together."

"Oh, I know that look." Steph pulled one of her legging-clad legs up into a stretch. Her muscles would be screaming after this workout. And the longer she could keep him talking, the less running they'd be doing. "That is the look of a man who is completely smitten with his fake fiancée."

"What are you..." Nick roughed his hand over his stubble-covered chin. "What does that even look like?"

"You." Steph switched legs and started to stretch out the other one. "It looks exactly like you. Don't deny it."

"Okay."

She dropped her leg and stared at her friend. "What? Are you serious?"

He shrugged.

"You *are* smitten with her? I thought it was all casual and easy. No expectations." She used air quotes with each description.

But Nick simply stared at her and shrugged again. "It was

supposed to be, but…" He looked down and shook his head. "I don't know how to explain it."

"Try."

Nick chuckled. "I think I'm falling in love with her."

His confession took her breath away. Sure, Steph had always kind of guessed that there was something between them. It was obvious just to look at the two of them that there was a connection of some kind. But *love*? That was unexpected.

"And what are you going to do about that?"

He gave her a sidelong look and scrubbed a hand through his hair, but before he could answer her, the watch on his wrist rang.

Steph muttered something about how annoying smart watches were and walked a few steps away to stretch her calf on the railing as Nick took the call. She didn't mean to listen in, but there was no way to avoid it.

"Hey, Char. What's—"

"She's here."

Charlotte's voice filled the air, and the panic laced in her words made Steph forget all about the calf stretch or the fact that she was trying not to eavesdrop. She turned and listened openly.

"Who's here?" Nick didn't bother trying to hide the concern in his voice. "Char? What's going on?"

"She's here," Charlotte said again. "Amelia's mother."

Just a few simple words and Steph's heart sank, just the way she knew Nick's was as well. But it was her next words that shot fear through her.

"She wants to take the baby."

The second her words registered in Stephanie's brain, she made eye contact with Nick, who had the same look on his face that she knew she must, and she sprang into action. It was just a quick sprint to where she left her bag, and Nick was right behind her.

"Put her off as long as you can, Char. We're on our way. It'll be okay."

Nick was talking to Charlotte, trying to keep her calm and figure out exactly what was going on while at the same time, Stephanie was already pulling out her cell phone to make the arrangements that would get them to Charlotte and Amelia as fast as possible.

It wasn't the first time that Stephanie had used her private helicopter to get her to Glacier Falls in a hurry, and despite the fact that the flight only took twenty minutes instead of the three-hour drive, it still took far too long. Nick could hardly be contained during the short flight. He spent most of the trip muttering, clenching and unclenching his fists, and texting his lawyer.

He filled her in on what the lawyer said. About how if Jessica checked out, they'd have to let her take the baby.

It was heart-breaking.

More than anything, Stephanie wished she could do something, anything to help her friend through the situation. But beyond supplying the mode of transport, there was nothing else she could do. And she'd never felt more helpless in her entire life than when she watched him run to the waiting car that would take him immediately to ElkView and his daughter.

Hopefully it wasn't too late.

It couldn't be. She couldn't let herself think that way.

Steph stood and stared down the road long after the SUV had driven away and the dust it kicked up had settled.

It was only then that she felt a total emptiness settle over her. She'd been alone a long time. Even when she'd been engaged to Dax Combs, she'd still been on her own most of the time. But never had she been *lonely*.

There was only one place that could give her the peace she needed. At least she hoped it could.

Stephanie thanked her helicopter pilot, and got in her own SUV to make the drive to Lynx Creek.

Just as she'd hoped, the moment she drove up the windy road to the old fishing camp, a sense of peace came over her. She went directly to Bankside, her cabin, and sat on the porch that faced the creek. She dangled her legs off the deck that didn't yet have its railing and tried to lose herself in the burbling of the water.

She'd told Nick to let her know as soon as something happened, but she didn't really expect to hear from him for a while. Maybe she should have gone to Ever After Ranch to be around her sisters, but Faith and Hope would only be worried as well and that would only make her feel worse. She tried to take a deep breath, but it hitched in her chest as a sob she'd been holding in escaped her lungs.

All the emotion she held for Nick and Amelia, and Charlotte, too, came busting out of her. Tears streaked down her face as she let herself ugly cry. With her shoulders shaking and her nose running, she let herself cry in a way like she'd never let herself go before. Before Glacier Falls and her cabins at Lynx Creek, it felt like there was always somebody watching her and a photographer waiting around every corner, ready to jump at the perfect shot of her doing something wrong, or looking wrong, or just living her life in a way that was tabloid-worthy.

But there was no one around now. Just her and the woods.

She let herself cry until, finally, there were no more tears and she dropped backward so she was lying on the wooden deck, flat on her back.

The moment she closed her eyes, a wet tongue licked at her face with the enthusiasm only a puppy could have.

Steph squealed and sat up, wrapping her arms around

Tinker Bell, who'd grown remarkably larger since she'd seen her last. "Oh my goodness." She laughed. "Aren't you the sweetest thing. And you've grown. You're going to be a big girl."

"Hey. Don't give her body issues."

Steph's head snapped up to see Travis, looking every bit as sexy as the last time she'd seen him. Only this time, he was once more dressed in his usual cowboy boots, worn jeans, and a T-shirt. He looked down at her with a cocky grin, but it dissolved into a frown of concern when he saw her.

"Hey." He crouched down so he was eye to eye with her. "What's wrong? I didn't mean to...are you okay, Steph?"

His voice was so tender, and the hand that reached out to wipe a lingering tear from her cheek was equally tender, that it caused a fresh round of tears to well up in her eyes.

Still with the puppy in her lap, Steph buried her face in Tinker Bell's fur. "No," she said. "I mean...yes. I'm fine." She looked up when he put his hand on her shoulder. "It's just a lot built up and...well...I think I'm lonely." It was the most simplistic thing she could think to say. But she couldn't bring herself to rehash everything with Nick and Char and the baby. Besides, she didn't know what she should say about that situation, so it was probably easier not to say anything. Besides, she *was* lonely. And when, a moment later, Travis moved so he sat next to her on the porch and slipped an arm over her shoulders as if it were the most natural thing in the whole world, she suddenly didn't feel quite so lonely anymore.

His arm was warm, and reflexively, she snuggled into him. Travis wrapped his other arm around her and stroked her hair while the puppy bounced around them and alternately licked at their hands and tried to bite at their clothes. Finally, Tinker Bell managed to get her tongue in her ear. Steph squealed and laughed and tried to pull away to wipe her ear, but Travis held her fast. When she turned to look at him in question, the intensity in his gaze took her breath away and the laughter died on her lips.

He shifted a little so he could put one hand on her cheek. Travis held her in place and lowered his face to hers in a kiss that erased every single trace of loneliness she'd ever felt in her entire life.

Chapter Fourteen

NO. *No. No.*

This wasn't happening. It couldn't be happening.

Charlotte worked hard to make the smile she'd pasted on her face look as natural as possible when she returned from the bedroom, where she'd called Nick in a panic.

She didn't want to worry him while he was in the city and so far away, but there was no other option. She was here. In their home. And she wanted their baby.

Their baby.

It was the first thought that popped into her head when the woman who'd introduced herself as Jessica said she was there for her daughter.

No.

Amelia was *her* daughter. And Nick's. Mostly Nick's. But still, Charlotte's too. Sort of. In a roundabout way.

But most certainly was *not* Jessica's daughter.

She'd given her up. She'd abandoned her. She couldn't have her back. Not just like that. Not if Charlotte had anything to say about it.

"Well?" Jessica turned around, her hair swinging behind her.

As much as Charlotte didn't want to notice—or care—she *really* didn't want to care—Jessica was pretty. She was petite, almost tiny. And she had a fragility about her. She wore very little makeup, which only made her look younger. And more innocent than she currently did. If it was even possible.

And Nick had been with her. They'd dated. Or not really, according to Nick. They weren't really in a relationship, but she had met when Nick was in his *party phase*, which had ended abruptly when Amelia came into his life. He'd told her that Jessica was still in that phase. A drug addict with no capacity to take care of a child. This woman in front of her didn't look like an addict. Sure, she looked tired and worn out, but that didn't make her unfit.

"Will Nick be home soon?" Jessica prodded when Charlotte didn't answer. "With Amelia?"

Charlotte had panicked when Jessica told her she was there for her baby, so she'd said the first thing she could think of: Nick had the baby with him in the city. She'd hoped that would be enough to get rid of her. It wasn't. She'd insisted on waiting.

"It could be a few hours," Char said. "I just spoke to him and he's changing his plans, but it'll take some time to get back home. It is a bit of a drive."

Jessica sat, uninvited, on the couch. "I'll wait." She offered Charlotte a small shrug. "I don't really have anywhere to go, you know? I just came for Amelia."

Again, Charlotte's gut clenched. And she was thankful she'd sent the baby with Katie. She'd be safe there and it would buy her some time before Nick got there. Thinking of Katie, she needed to text her to let her know that—

"Are you Nick's girlfriend?"

Jessica's question distracted her, and Charlotte put her cell phone back in her pocket. Maybe if she could convincingly play the role of fiancée and devoted stepmother, Jessica would get scared off? Maybe she'd realize that her baby was better off with her and Nick, and she could get rid of her before Nick even got home?

It was a huge long shot, but she didn't have anything else, and she needed to do something. She felt so helpless, just waiting.

"I'm actually his fiancée." She pressed her lips together. "We're just so in love, it's been really great." She sat next to Jessica on the couch. "I really don't know where I'd be if I hadn't met him. It's like we were meant to be, you know?" She hated the way her voice dripped with over-the-top sweetness. But she needed this woman to understand that she and Nick were unbreakable. She couldn't sweep in and—

"I think that's great." Jessica nodded a little as she smiled. "Are you two going to have children of your own?"

The question took her off guard, but she recovered quickly. "I think Amelia will be a fabulous big sister, so I would love to give her a little brother or sister as soon as possible."

Jessica's smile dropped and her face screwed up into a frown.

Yes. Charlotte did a silent cheer. That had done it. *Jessica would see that they were a perfect family and Amelia belonged with them, and—*

"I think you might be confused," Jessica said slowly.

"Confused?" Charlotte chuckled and shook her head. "I don't think so. We are going to have children."

"Amelia is *my* daughter." Jessica's voice took on an edge. "She's not yours."

Charlotte's spine stiffened. "I mean, I know she's not mine by birth." She worked hard to control her voice. "But, I love her as if she's my own. And any child of Nick's is—"

"That's just it." Jessica interrupted. "I thought you knew. Amelia isn't Nick's daughter."

ELENA AITKEN

Something close to rage boiled through her, but somehow Charlotte managed to contain herself. "What I *know* is that Nick is an amazing father to that baby. He hasn't hesitated to jump in and raise her. He's given up everything for her, and that is what a father is. It doesn't matter one bit if he isn't biologically Amelia's father. He's been working hard to do whatever he can to make sure that Amelia's needs come first and that the decisions that are made are in Amelia's best interest."

Jessica didn't say anything for a moment, but she recovered quickly. "Well," she said with a grin. "If Nick is so worried about what's best for Amelia, he'll have already told you that what's best for Amelia has already been decided."

What? Nick hadn't said a word to her about it. Charlotte swallowed hard, unwilling to show this woman that she'd gotten to her.

"And *it has* been decided," Jessica continued. "Amelia will be leaving with me. Her mother."

Charlotte worked hard to remember the breath work her therapist had taught her, but it was all she could do to simply get air in and out of her lungs to keep breathing. Somehow she managed to pull one breath in and then another but oxygen was still having trouble reaching her brain, because she was sure she'd heard Jessica say that she'd be taking Amelia. That it had been *decided*.

"Pardon me?" Charlotte interrupted. "Did you just say that—"

Jessica cut her off with a nod. "I'm not sure what Nick told you about me, but I'm willing to bet it had everything to do with my past and not my present."

Charlotte shook her head in disbelief.

"And yes, I left her with him. Who wouldn't? I mean, there could have been a chance that he was the father. He's not," she added pointedly. "But who wouldn't want a billionaire to be the father of their baby, right?"

She laughed a little, but there was nothing humorous about it. *This couldn't be real. This woman couldn't be real. The things she was saying...*

"Anyway...my lawyer...well, he's not *my* lawyer, but he's legal aid, and he said that Nick had applied for adoption and there's no way. So I'm here to take her back."

"*Take her back?*" Charlotte repeated. "That's not how it works." She knew she shouldn't say anything to aggravate the woman, but she couldn't stop herself. "Whatever you think you know, Nick is Amelia's father and very clearly the best parent for her." She raised her eyebrows. She knew all about Jessica's substance abuse and her history. In any other situation, she would have felt like a grade-A bitch, but all bets were off if it meant protecting what was hers. And as unconventional as it was, Nick and Amelia were *hers.*

"But he's not the parent," Jessica said. "And you both clearly know it."

"That doesn't matter. You're—"

"It *does* matter," Jessica said. "Quite a bit, actually. Which is why I'm here."

"But you're an..."

"Addict?" Jessica finished for her. She shut her eyes for a moment and when she opened them, they focused like lasers on Charlotte. "I am. I was. I...it's a constant work in progress," she said, as if it were part of a rehearsed script. "I work at it every day. For Amelia. I do it for her."

"But you—"

"I'm clean. Nine weeks now. Not that I need to explain this to you. Nick should have told you already. I mean, since you're his fiancée and all. I assume he would have told you that I'd be coming."

He knew. Nick knew this woman would be coming into their house and taking their baby. He knew and he hadn't told her.

Their house. Their baby.

But that was the thing: it wasn't real. None of it. And despite how Charlotte's feelings had changed, it was clear that Nick's hadn't. Not only that, he didn't even think enough of her to warn her that this was going to happen.

She wanted to throw up. She wanted to run away and hide.

Instead, Charlotte dropped her head and stared at her hands in her lap. Her fingers were twisted together. The ruby ring stuck out and sparkled in the light, but instead of admiring it the way she usually did, now it felt wrong. Everything felt wrong. She glanced at the clock on the wall. Nick would still be at least another ten minutes. If they'd gotten on the helicopter right away. Another detail she hadn't shared with Jessica.

But it looked as though she wasn't the only one holding back details.

"I know you're probably—"

"Knock knock."

Charlotte spun around and dashed to the door, but it was too late. Katie was already walking in, the way she always did. Only she had the baby on her hip. Charlotte's heart fell and clenched all at once.

"Sorry to interrupt," Katie said, with no idea what she'd just walked into. "Amelia desperately needs a diaper change and there weren't any left in the diaper bag. I think it's those peaches you've been feeding her and—"

Char tried to distract her and get Katie turned around. "I can just—"

"Is that…"

Too late.

"Amelia?" Jessica's voice cracked on the baby's name.

Char dropped her head and squeezed her eyes shut for a moment. When she opened them, Katie's eyes were wide with shock and concern. She held onto Amelia a little tighter, a fact that Charlotte was more than grateful for.

"Oh my God. Amelia," Jessica cried. "My baby."

Char instinctively stepped between Jessica and Amelia. There was no way she was letting this woman take Amelia. Not like this.

It felt like it took hours, but thanks to Stephanie's helicopter, it had only been a fraction of that time. Still, Nick had spent every second of that time trying not to picture what would happen when he got there.

Jessica wanted the baby. She wanted *his* daughter. There was no way...he couldn't let it happen. But Chris's words replayed in his mind. *Play nice. It's her right.*

Nick had reached out to Chris on the flight over, and he'd expressed his concern, but at the same time, had told Nick exactly what he didn't want to hear. She had a clean drug test. If Jessica wanted to take the baby, he wouldn't be able to stop her. And, in fact, might only do more harm than good to securing custody long-term.

He'd tried calling Susan Johnson at least four times, but there'd been no answer.

It didn't make sense. The system was broken. Hell, it was completely shattered. Any system that thought it was perfectly okay for a woman who'd abandoned her child to have any right to walk back into the child's life at her own convenience and disrupt everything was not okay.

Not that he had any choice but to play along.

Or did he?

He shook his head and took a deep breath as the car pulled

into the ElkView Ridge drive. He needed to pull it together, and think with his brain, not his heart. He needed to do what was best for Amelia in the long run. He'd promised Chris he wouldn't do anything rash or illegal.

He was out of the car before it had come to a complete stop and at the front door. He sucked in a breath as he opened the door, not sure what he was going to see. "I got here as soon as I…"

His words trailed off as he took in the scene inside.

Katie had the baby in her arms. Charlotte stood with her back to them both, her arms crossed over her chest as she stood guard between the baby and Jessica, who had tears in her eyes as she clearly was trying to get to Amelia.

Nick's chest constricted at what he was witnessing. He had no feelings toward Jessica, none that were caring or loving, at any rate. Their relationship hadn't been more than partying and hooking up. There'd been no emotional connection at all. In fact, he hadn't even known her last name until recently. Yet, he couldn't help but feel a twinge of…something…as he set eyes on her again after so long. She was, after all, Amelia's mother, and he loved that little girl more than anything in the world. The only thing he'd ever felt toward Jessica was anger that she could leave her baby, but now… *No.* He needed to remember the anger. *This woman left her child. She was an addict. She was unfit.*

Katie half turned to Nick. Her eyes were wide with worry and relief to see him, as if he could fix the situation.

Maybe he could. Or at any rate, maybe he could deescalate it so that it worked out for Amelia. He nodded a thank-you to Katie and took Amelia, who had her arms outstretched to him, from his friend.

"I'm going to get Damon," Katie whispered as she slipped from the guest house.

But Nick didn't respond. He was focused on the other two women in the room.

"Tell this woman that she will not be taking our baby today." Char didn't even glance in his direction as she spoke to him through gritted teeth.

"Char." He spoke her name gently as he came to stand next to her. He took his free hand and reached for hers. He gave it a squeeze until she looked at him.

"Tell her, Nick." Charlotte's voice shook a little.

He knew she'd hate that. But she was going to hate it even more that he couldn't tell her what she wanted to hear. He inhaled the sweet scent of Amelia's shampoo and kissed her on her head. An action that almost brought him to tears. *How was he supposed to let Jessica take her?*

"She's Amelia's mother," he said, simply. "Why don't we all sit down and discuss a few things."

Charlotte's eyes opened in disbelief, as if she couldn't believe he'd even suggest anything besides kicking Jessica out on her ass—which, admittedly, was exactly what he wanted to do. It was taking all of his self-control to do the *right* thing. Even if it felt anything but right.

"Nick?"

Slowly, Nick met Jessica's eyes that were so much like her daughter's that it was startling. He held the baby a little tighter.

"Can I hold her, Nick?"

She twisted her hands together and leaned forward a little as she spoke, as if she was being drawn to the baby in a physical way.

Nick swallowed hard. "Why don't we sit down for a minute and…" He looked at Char. "Can you please take Amelia for a quick diaper change?"

Thankfully, Char nodded and took the baby. She held her tight and glared at Jessica as she disappeared into the bedroom.

They didn't speak at all while Charlotte was gone, and as

soon as she returned with a freshened-up Amelia, Nick once more took the baby. He tried to give Charlotte a reassuring smile, but her mouth was set in a fixed line.

"Why don't we all sit down for a minute?" he suggested.

As soon as everyone was seated, somewhat awkwardly on the sofa, Nick was out of excuses.

"Please, Nick?" Jessica asked again. "Can I hold my daughter?"

Next to him, Charlotte made a snorting noise, and if he wasn't mistaken, a low growl rumbled from her. He squeezed her thigh briefly in an effort to settle her, but it wasn't going to be that easy.

"There's no way you're going to let her hold her, Nick." She didn't even bother trying to lower her voice. "She doesn't deserve it, Nick. You can't—"

"She's Amelia's mother, Char. I have to—"

"You're her *father*, Nick. That counts, too."

She looked at him imploring him to make it all better. But he couldn't. And she didn't even know the half of it, a fact that killed him a little inside.

"I'm sorry, Char."

She tore her eyes from his and looked away as he handed Amelia to Jessica, because it was the right thing to do. But again, the *right thing* felt so fucking wrong.

The moment Nick handed Jessica the baby, he wanted her back. His arms were empty and his breath was tight in his lungs. Next to him, Charlotte was tense and didn't take her eyes off Jessica, who didn't appear to notice Charlotte's animosity, or more likely, didn't care. Because she had her baby in her arms.

Nick watched closely as Jessica used her finger to trace

Amelia's face, touching first her cheek, then her nose and her chin.

"She's so gorgeous," Jessica said, more to herself than anyone else.

Charlotte made a choking, sobbing noise and Nick reached for her hand. "How could you let her...she's *your* daughter, Nick."

"I told you." Jessica looked up, her face cold and her eyes narrow as she fixed them on Charlotte. "Nick isn't her father."

His breath caught in his chest.

"What?" Jessica continued. "You didn't think I knew who my baby's father was?"

He shook his head slowly. Of course, he'd had his suspicions that she'd figured it out. After all, he didn't know much about it all, but he'd assumed a woman usually had a pretty good idea about who the father of their baby was. That being said, when her sister had shown up with Amelia in her arms and dropped her into his life with the announcement that she was his daughter, Nick had just thought Jessica was too messed up to know who the baby's father really was and she'd picked the best option. And without even knowing who the other options were, he *knew* he was the best one. He had to be.

"I wasn't sure," he finally said. "And there's a chance that..." He drifted off because they both knew the chance that Amelia was biologically his was slim, to say the least.

"I'm here to take her home."

Next to him, Charlotte tensed. "This *is* her home. You have no right to take her." Charlotte turned to him with so much hope in her eyes, something inside him died a little. "Tell her, Nick. Tell her she can't take Amelia."

"He can't." Jessica chuckled. "Because he knows that legally I can take her. And I am."

"He doesn't know that." Char looked between them, the panic rising in her. "Do you, Nick? You didn't know..."

Her eyes darkened, and Nick could see the moment she realized the truth. He *had* known. And he hadn't told her. He'd never warned her about what could happen. What *was* happening.

"I'm so sorry, Char."

He turned to her and tried to take her hand in his, but the damage had already been done and she pulled away.

"I didn't want to believe it," she said slowly.

Her voice was thick with emotion. He'd done that to her. It was his fault that she was fighting back tears. And he hated himself for it.

"She told me you knew all this was happening. But I couldn't believe that you'd know such a thing and not tell me. That you'd let me…" She swallowed back a sob.

"Char." He reached for her hands, taking them both in his. "I was going to fix it. I was going to—"

"Rip my heart out," she finished for him.

He nodded because there was nothing else he could do. "I'm so sorry."

"How could you…" Charlotte dropped her head.

Nick swallowed hard.

"After everything…I would have…" After a moment, she looked up, first to Nick and then to Jessica, who was holding Amelia, but looking straight at Charlotte with what could only be described as a smirk on her face.

"Thanks for taking care of her for me." Jessica's voice dripped with insincerity. "But I'll take it from here."

This time, Nick was positive it was a growl that came from Charlotte, and he held her fast so she didn't jump up. He didn't think that Char would attack the other woman, but at the same time, he had no idea what a woman backed into a corner would do.

"It's okay," Nick said. He didn't even believe what he was saying. "We need to let her—"

"No." Char tore her hands out of his and crossed her arms over her chest. "It's *not* okay."

Nick sighed. Never in his life had he longed for backup more than in that moment. "Can I talk to you for a minute?" He stood and reached a hand out to Charlotte.

She didn't take it, but stood on her own and walked into the attached kitchen. Her eyes never left Jessica and Amelia once.

"Char, I'm—"

"You can't let her take the baby, Nick." She interrupted him. "You can't."

He swallowed hard. "My hands are tied, Char. I have to—"

"Your hands are tied?" She glared at him and it killed him inside that he'd hurt her so badly but despite how he'd behaved, she was still willing to be there for him, and more importantly, Amelia. "How can you say that? After everything. The lies, the deceit, and *now* you're saying your hands are tied?" She choked on a laugh and shook her head.

"Charlotte, I'm so sorry." He tried to reach for her, but she pulled away.

"Don't apologize, Nick." When she turned back to him, her eyes shone with unshed tears. "Not to me." She bit her bottom lip. "You need to apologize to that little girl in there. Because..." Her words were lost on a sob. He waited while she took in a deep breath. She opened her mouth, but closed it again and shook her head.

There were no words that could have possibly cut him deeper than the way she looked at him in that moment.

Charlotte turned and walked across the room so she stood in front of Jessica and Amelia, who started to fuss. The baby reached for Charlotte and smiled when she saw her. Charlotte reached out a finger and Amelia instantly wrapped a chubby fist tightly around it. Tears fell down Charlotte's face as she looked at the baby, trying to communicate in a simple touch.

It was such a sweet moment, hot tears pricked at Nick's eyes.

A sob escaped Charlotte and an instant later, Jessica yanked Amelia away. The baby cried in protest and Jessica immediately started patting her back and bouncing her, causing the baby to cry harder.

Nick moved instinctively toward Amelia, and he saw that Char had moved to do the same, but she caught herself before reaching out. Instead, she again wrapped her arms around her waist, turned to look at Nick with tears streaming down her face, shook her head, turned, and ran out of the guest house.

Chapter Fifteen

CHARLOTTE DIDN'T KNOW where to go but she knew she couldn't stay at the house. She couldn't stand by while Nick just handed over Amelia to a total stranger. *A total stranger who had abandoned her baby once before. An addict. A…*

It didn't matter that Jessica was her mother. Not to Charlotte. It took more than blood and DNA to be a mother. And maybe everyone deserved a second chance, but Charlotte could not bring herself to think that way. Not yet. Not like this. Not when it came to Amelia.

She deserved better.

Char drove her car through a veil of tears, down the winding roads. She couldn't go to her parents or to Jeremy. How could she admit that she'd been so very wrong? She'd basically insisted that they trust her instincts on this, that she was doing the right thing. *Her instincts?* What a joke. Obviously she couldn't trust her gut. Not when she'd been so sure that Nick was an amazing father who'd do anything for his little girl.

He wouldn't protect her now, and she couldn't stand by and watch it happen.

She'd been so wrong.

The reality of it all hit her like a brick. She'd twisted her entire life up for him. The lying and acting and...*falling.* She'd totally fallen for him, and none of it had been true. She'd been so stupid to let herself think it could be anything. That it *was* anything. When obviously he didn't consider her the same way. Hell, he didn't consider her at all if he couldn't be bothered to tell her what was going to happen.

Clearly, she wasn't nearly as ready to move on from her past as she'd thought. She couldn't trust her gut then, and it was painfully obvious, she couldn't trust it now.

She swallowed back another sob.

The pain in her chest was almost too much to bear. A double whammy. She'd fallen in love with both of them—Nick and Amelia. And she'd fallen hard. And now...

Charlotte wasn't sure where she was going, until she turned down the road that would lead to Lynx Creek.

The cabins.

Surely, Stephanie wouldn't mind if she stayed for a little bit in one of the cabins. She just needed a bit of time. Some space before going...well, she'd figure that out after.

She drove up the hill, toward the cabin that she'd been working on last. The *Lumberjack* cabin. It was the most private. She'd be able to cry and feel sorry for herself in peace.

Char ignored her ringing phone as she parked her car behind the little cabin. Whoever it was, she didn't want to talk to them. She had nothing to say to Nick and everyone else... she didn't feel like talking. She needed to be left alone so she could pull her thoughts together and figure out what she was going to do and where she was going to go. Her heart hurt way too much to formulate a reasonable thought of any kind. What she really needed was a good cry.

And that's just what she did. She left her phone in the car, and didn't even bother opening the front door to the cabin.

Instead, she dropped to the porch floor and pulled her legs up into her chest, tucked her head down and cried for everything that had just happened and all the things that she couldn't even begin to understand.

She'd been so stupid letting her guard down again for Nick.

He was different.

Wrong.

He wasn't different. He was another man who filled her with lies to get what he wanted from her. He'd used her and worse, he'd made her fall in love with him.

Fall in love.

Shit.

Yes. *Love.* It was the last thing she'd wanted to happen and the exact opposite of what was *supposed* to happen. No expectations, right?

So much for that.

She'd fallen hard. *Really* hard.

And not just for him.

It was too much. She needed to stop thinking. She needed to numb it. Shut it off. She needed—

Alcohol.

There was a bottle of Prosecco in the cabin from when Nick had surprised her the day of the caseworker visit. With everything that had happened, she'd forgotten all about it. She meant to take it back to the house for them to drink there, but she hadn't gotten around to it.

Perfect.

Slowly, Charlotte pulled herself up from the porch and without bothering to dust herself off, dug the keys out of her pocket.

But the door to the cabin was unlocked. She held her hand on the doorknob for a moment before turning it. *Had she left it unlocked the last time she was there?*

It had been a few days since she'd been up to the cabin and

she couldn't remember locking the door, but she always did. *Maybe Travis had opened it? For the furniture delivery?*

Yes. The furniture she'd ordered was supposed to be delivered.

Charlotte shook her head at her own forgetfulness. If she wasn't careful, she'd lose this job and then she'd really have nothing left. Maybe Nick had turned out to be…well, at least she had her career. That's what she'd do. Focus on her career. All in. *Maybe then she could—*

Two steps into the cabin, Charlotte froze.

Someone had been there.

And not to deliver furniture.

The small space was still empty. Almost exactly how she'd left it the last time she'd been there. *Almost.*

There were dark, muddy footprints on the pine floorboards.

She sucked in a breath and turned slowly.

The bottle of bubbly she'd left on the cupboard had been opened. A paper cup sat next to it. Splashes of wine dotted the countertop.

This is wrong.

She tried not to jump to conclusions, but her instincts knew better. Icy fear ran through her veins and up her spine.

Run, a voice deep inside her screamed at her.

She needed to get out of there. Quickly.

Charlotte darted for the only exit, but it was too late. A man stepped through the door and closed it behind him.

Billy.

Amelia had stopped crying. Finally.

It had taken Nick over twenty minutes to calm her down after Charlotte left. She was finally bouncing in her play saucer and giggling at the various toys he'd put in place to distract her. Poor kid was no doubt picking up on his tension as well as the fact that a strange woman had been holding her. But she wasn't a stranger; she was her *mother.* Nick had to continually remind himself of that.

Jessica was her mother.

He wasn't even her father.

It ate him up to even think that. But at the same time, it was the only way he was going to be able to do what he knew he had to do.

But it didn't matter how many times he'd called Chris; that was his professional advice. "If she wants to take the baby, you have to let her, Nick. Legally. We'll fight it. We'll do everything we can, but we have to do it by the book."

By the book.

Nothing about this situation was by the book. They were rewriting the whole goddamned book, and there was nothing he could do.

"I've put in a call to your caseworker," Chris said on their last call. "Susan Johnson. To see if there's anything else we can do. Something I missed. I'm still waiting for her to call me back. But, Nick? I didn't miss anything. You'll have to let her go."

Finally, he couldn't put it off any longer. It was getting late. Jessica was getting restless. She was ready to go.

"Don't do this, Jessica." He tried one final plea. "Let's talk about it and—"

"She's *my* daughter, Nick. Thank you for taking care of her, but I'm better now and I want her back."

Want her back? She wasn't some *thing* that could be cast aside and called back on a whim. She was a *child.* This wasn't right.

Nick bit back his words and swallowed hard.

"There's a reason you left her with me, Jessica. You know I

can give her a good life. I can give her—" His voice cracked with emotion. "Don't do this."

She didn't even have the decency to look remorseful. Instead, she just shook her head sadly. "I'm doing this, Nick. I'm her mother. She belongs with me. Are her things packed?"

"I didn't have a chance to—"

"Never mind." Jessica walked past him to where Amelia was playing. As Jessica grew closer, the baby started to fuss. "I'll get new stuff. I just want to get out of here." She turned to the little girl. "Come on, kiddo. It's time to get out of here."

Panic filled Nick. A helplessness like nothing he'd ever felt before rose up through him. His heart raced. Sweat beaded along his hairline. "Where are you staying? Do you have a place nearby? It's getting late to go to—"

"I got a place, Nick. It's fine."

"Where is it? I can—"

"I told you." She glared at him. "It's fine." She swooped Amelia up out of the play saucer and Amelia started to cry almost at once.

Nick winced and moved to grab the baby. "Just let me—"

Jessica swung around to keep him away. "No." Her voice was firm, with an edge that hadn't been there before. "Look, Nick. I know you got attached to her, but she's not your daughter and you know that. Legally, I can do this. And I've been more than patient about it. Let it go."

Let it go?

He couldn't just let it go. Let *her* go.

Amelia's cries grew louder, as if she sensed that what was about to happen was not okay. It wasn't. Nothing about it was okay. Jessica pushed past him to the door. It took every bit of self-restraint not to stop her.

It will only make things worse. Play nice.

Nick swallowed hard. He'd do things by the book. He

wouldn't do anything to screw up his chances at getting custody.

He followed her outside. "I'll fight you, Jessica," he said as she buckled Amelia into the car seat. His heart was being ripped out of his body with every cry. He clenched each hand into a tight fist and willed himself not to cry. Or throw himself on the car. "I love that little girl, and I will do everything in my power to get her back."

She finished strapping in the baby and looked Nick in the eye.

"This isn't over, Jessica."

She didn't say a word as she got in the car and drove away with a piece of his heart, crying in the backseat.

Despite his vow, he couldn't help but feel that he'd been wrong. Because it very much felt over. All of it.

Chapter Sixteen

HE STOOD in the dust cloud Jessica's car left behind long enough for the dust to settle and erase any traces of the car that had just taken his little girl away. Never in his life, in all the times he'd been on his own, had Nick ever felt so completely alone. In one afternoon, he'd lost both Charlotte and Amelia.

There was nothing left.

"Fuck!"

Anger washed through him with such a force, it took him completely off guard and left him dizzy with rage. He strode toward a pine tree, pulled back, and punched it as hard as he could. The pain screamed through his fist, but he ignored it and hit the tree again.

"Nick!"

Damon grabbed him by the shoulders and pulled him back, away from the tree, but the anger wasn't yet satisfied. He spun to throw a punch at Damon. Cocked his fist and froze at his best friend's undefended face.

He was about to punch his best friend and Damon wasn't even going to stop him because he knew he needed the release.

The reality of the entire situation hit him. He dropped his arm as his shoulders slumped and a sob ripped from deep in his chest.

Without missing a beat, Damon pulled him in and hugged him hard.

It didn't take long for the anger and anguish to subside enough for Nick to allow Damon to lead him into the main house, where he set a glass of water in front of him and sat across from him at the kitchen island. Katie had appeared with a wet towel and gently, without asking, took Nick's hand and started cleaning the cuts.

"What can we do?"

Nick dropped his chin to his chest. "Nothing."

"I don't believe that, Nick." Damon shook his head. "It's not like you to just give up. You *never* give up. There's a problem, you solve it. So let's—"

"We can't." He jerked his hand away from Katie and immediately felt bad. "Sorry."

"It's fine." She smiled kindly, and took it back and resumed washing the cuts.

"We can't solve this," Nick said to Damon. "I've been talking to Chris, and he says we have to play by the rules on this one. She's not biologically my daughter and that means I have no rights. It's so fucked up."

"That *is* fucked up. There has to be something they're missing. You can't just give a child back to the parent who abandoned her like she was nothing."

Damon's words hit him like fresh punches in the gut.

"It's not right. What did the caseworker say?"

"Chris is waiting to hear back, and I left a message, too. But Jessica has a clean drug test and…" The visit with Susan Johnson had gone so well, she had to be on their side as far as custody went. It was her job to do what was in the best interest of the child. Surely she'd see that what was in Amelia's best interest was him and Charlotte. *They* were what was best. And —*Charlotte*. She'd left. She was so hurt. So angry. And… Nick looked at Katie. "Charlotte left."

Katie nodded. "I know."

"Do you know where she went?"

Katie shook her head and, finished with his hand, which was now throbbing, released it with a gentle pat.

"She hates me."

"I'm sure she doesn't hate you," Katie said. "She's hurt and confused."

"I've screwed everything up so badly." He wanted to hit something again but the pain in his fist reminded him why that wasn't likely a good idea. He was lucky it wasn't broken. Even if it was, he didn't care. He didn't care about anything without Amelia and Charlotte.

"I'm going to call Remington." Damon pushed away from the counter with sudden force. "He's an old friend from school," he explained as he pulled his cell phone out. "He's a cop in town and…well, I don't know what he can do. But maybe he can at least keep an eye out for Jessica's car and…"

Nick nodded. It was something. "Call him."

A few minutes later, Damon was off the phone. "Okay. Remi is going to keep an eye out for the car. He'll let us know if he sees anything, and as soon as he locates her, he'll keep a tail on her as much as he can. It's not much, but…"

"It's better than nothing." Nick nodded. "And it's a whole lot better than what I'm doing." He couldn't sit any longer. "I need to go after her."

"Who?"

He stopped. His hands might be tied when it came to Amelia. He'd take Chris's advice because he didn't want to screw it up. He'd play by the rules, even if it went against everything he thought was right. But he'd do it for Amelia. He had to.

But Charlotte...there *was* something he could do to fix that. Hopefully. She'd been hurt before. Badly. And she'd trusted him. He'd betrayed that trust and he'd spend the rest of his life making amends for that if she'd let him. But first...he needed to find her.

"I need to find Charlotte," he told his friends. "I need to tell her everything."

"Nick?" Katie stopped him, confusion on her face. "Isn't that why she left?" she asked. "Because she knows everything now?"

"No." He shook his head. "She doesn't know how much I love her."

Charlotte backed up into the cabin. Her pulse thundered in her ears, making it hard to think straight.

Billy?

Her brain just couldn't wrap around the fact that she was looking at her ex-boyfriend, the one she'd left on the other side of the country in a stealth-like mission, sneaking away and leaving everything behind.

And he was here.

Here.

If anyone asked, she told them she had never been afraid of Billy. Not really. He'd only gotten physical with her a few times, but only when he'd been drinking and even then, she wasn't scared. *Not really.*

But she'd been scared enough that Jeremy had helped her get away from him. Distance had made her complacent. She'd forgotten how imposing he could be. How threatening he could be without even saying a word.

It was all coming back. Quickly.

"What are you doing here?"

"I'm here for you." He stepped inside the cabin and shut the door behind him as he leaned back against it. "I've been watching and waiting, Char. It's hard to get you alone."

Alone.

She was alone.

But had he been watching her…

"How did you know where to find me?"

He laughed.

It was a chilling noise that made her stomach turn.

"You didn't think I'd know where you went?" He shook his head. "You never could stop talking about your stupid hometown and once I got here…well, it's not like you've been hiding. Hanging all over that guy. Playing house with his baby."

He snorted in disgust, but Char was focused on what he'd just said. He'd been watching her. He'd seen her. With Amelia. *What if…*

No. She couldn't let herself think about what would have happened if he'd gotten her alone with the baby. She needed to focus.

"It was a long drive, that's for sure." Billy was still talking. "But you're worth it, Char. I wasn't going to let you go that easy."

The hair on the back of her neck stood up. *Let you go that easy.* Char refused to let him see her panic.

"I drove a long way to see you, Charlotte. That's how much I love you."

No no no no. She couldn't let him trap her inside the cabin. She needed to get away.

"I miss you," he continued. "You left without even saying good-bye, Charlotte. Do you know how that made me feel?"

No. And she didn't care.

"But you came…why are you…" She needed to calm

down. She couldn't hold a thought, let alone think about what she was going to do.

"Charlotte. I asked you a question." His eyes darkened as he stepped closer.

That was the controlling, intimidating man she remembered. An involuntary shiver ran through her.

No.

She would not let him do this again. She would not so quickly fall into the trap of feeling like a small, useless person just because he needed a power trip.

No.

But there was something else in his eyes. Her eyes shot over to the counter where the Prosecco bottle and the paper cup sat. He'd been drinking. He almost never drank. He had no tolerance and it never ended well.

"Charlotte?" He stepped closer and that's when she saw it. The gleam of metal tucked into his waistband.

A gun.

Billy didn't own a gun. He wasn't the type. But then again, she didn't think he was the type to drive across the country to find her, either. She'd terribly underestimated him.

"I asked you a question."

She needed to think. But the only thing that came to mind was playing his game. Reverting to the scared, weak woman she'd been. The woman she'd hated. "I'm sorry, Billy." She lowered her eyes, the way she knew he'd prefer. *Don't look directly in his eye. Don't challenge him. Be submissive.* "I should have thought about how that would make you feel. It was a last-minute trip," she lied. "I needed to see my family and then I was going to—"

"Don't lie to me."

Her eyelids fluttered and she looked up. He wasn't buying it. He was drunk. He was close enough now to see the glassiness in his eyes.

Shit.

Quickly, she scanned the little cabin, and her eyes landed on the antique ax she'd bought to hang on the wall. She looked away before he could notice. If she could make it past him to the ax, she could—what? Hit him with it? It was heavy. Really heavy. But not impossibly so. She'd swung it the other day. Maybe she could knock him out, or at least stun him long enough to get away. She'd left her phone in the car. If she could get to it, she could call for help. But that would only work if she could get to the ax.

And there was only one way she could think to do that.

Char took a deep breath and exhaled slowly as she stepped toward Billy. "I really am sorry," she started. "It was a mistake. I never should have left. It's horrible here, and I miss you every day." It was so much bullshit, but she prayed that he didn't see through it, or remember the way she'd hung up on him when he'd called—repeatedly. She lifted a hand and reached out to touch his chest. She pressed her hand gently against his heart and looked up, just a little. "Can you ever forgive me?"

Charlotte licked her lips a little and tried to control the violent shivering that threatened to give her away. She just needed to distract him for one minute. *Just long enough to—*

"You're sorry?"

She swallowed hard, and tried not to cringe as Billy grabbed her chin roughly.

"I am." She nodded. "So sorry."

He kissed her roughly, and Char had to swallow back the bile that rose in her throat when he jabbed his tongue into her mouth.

Focus. Focus.

She returned the kiss just enough that Billy would be distracted as she moved closer to him—and the ax. Slowly, she kept his focus on her as she moved a little more to the left, closer still.

Charlotte prayed she had the location right. She couldn't afford to look. It would give her away, so hope was all she had.

She had to take the chance. She couldn't wait any longer.

Without overthinking it, Charlotte wrenched away from him and lunged for the ax. She raised it up quickly over her head. Adrenaline flowed through her veins, making the ax weightless in her grip as she turned around to face him.

And the gun he had pointed at her.

She didn't hesitate. She couldn't. She took a step and swung.

The gunshot blasted through the air, deafening her, and a white-hot pain sliced through her abdomen.

Her arms reverberated from the contact the ax made before it fell to the ground and her entire body went numb, the pain gone as she, too, fell to the ground.

Nick had spent the last twenty minutes calling Charlotte's phone continuously as he drove through the streets of Glacier Falls, but he couldn't find her or her car anywhere. He'd driven past her parents' home, before stopping at Jeremy's apartment, and even the fire hall.

No Charlotte.

He told them the truth, that they'd had an argument and she wasn't answering her phone, but he refused to get into any more details than that.

Where could she be?

The town wasn't that big. She couldn't have gone far.

Unless she went to the city?

But that didn't feel right. Charlotte was upset with him, certainly. And he deserved it. But she wouldn't have gone far. She would have gone somewhere where she could be alone. But—

His thoughts were interrupted by the ringing of his phone. He pulled over and reached for the phone. "Charlotte? Where are—"

"Nick? It's Susan," the caller interrupted him. "Susan Johnson. I'm returning your call."

It took him a moment to refocus his thoughts. "Right. Thank you."

"I was in a home visit, and I don't usually have my phone on during visits."

"I understand." He didn't mean to sound impatient, but there was a lot going on. "I was hoping that—"

"Right." She cut him off. "I wouldn't normally return your call so late, but when I got your message, I was concerned."

"Concerned?" He sat up in his seat.

"Yes," she continued. "Your lawyer also called and explained that Jessica had come for the baby."

Just hearing her say the words out loud caused a fresh wave of pain to wash through him. *The baby.* His baby. "She did." He could hear the defeat in his own voice. "And Chris told me that I needed to play nice and do things by the book. She's been clean and since she is Amelia's biological mother—"

"Right. That's why I'm calling."

Nick was on high alert.

"She had filed all of the appropriate information with child services, including recent drug tests and her sponsor's information. The follow-up is…well, I'll get to the point. There was a note in her file that her sponsor had some concerns."

Concerns?

"What kind of concerns?" He worked hard to stay calm. But he was quickly losing the battle. "Susan, talk to me. What kind of concerns are there about Jessica? She *has* Amelia."

"She does?"

Fuck.

"I would have recommended against returning the child to her biological mother at this point."

"What the—we were told she checked out. My lawyer checked it out. How could this happen?" He inhaled sharply.

"I don't know, Nick. Her legal aid...well, I don't know what else to say. But when I saw the file, I was—"

"Is she in danger?"

There was a hesitancy on the other end of the line, and it was all Nick needed to know.

"Off the record, Nick?"

He waited.

"I know what the law says, but if I were you..."

"That's all I needed to hear."

He ended the call and immediately dialed Damon. "We need to find her, now. Tell me Remi located them."

"I was about to call you." Damon sighed. "Remi said his contact reported seeing her."

"His contact?"

"A dealer. He's known to the cops."

"Wait. A dealer? As in drugs?" Nick was going to throw up. "But she's clean. She—"

"Not anymore, apparently."

"Fuck." *What had he done?*

"That was about an hour ago. Last she was spotted, she was headed through town on the road that leads up to Lynx Creek."

"Lynx Creek?"

Charlotte. The cabins. Lynx Creek.

"I'm on my way," he said. "I think Charlotte's probably out there, too."

"Char? Why would she—"

"I'm at least fifteen minutes away. Dammit. Meet me there. And call Steph. Maybe she's out there."

Open your eyes.

Open your eyes.

They were so heavy. It took all her effort to open her eyes, and when she did, she immediately wanted to close them again.

Blood. So much blood.

And Billy. He was lying on the cabin floor. *Was he dead?* Surely she hadn't hit him that hard.

The gunshot.

Slowly, Charlotte brought her hand to her right side and pulled it away, covered in blood. *Oh my God.*

She had to move. If Billy wasn't dead, he would wake up, and she couldn't be there. She needed to get to her phone.

Slowly, she managed to pull herself to her feet. She used the wall for balance as she moved as quickly as she could to the door.

The fresh air felt like freedom and she almost sagged to the ground in relief, but she wasn't safe yet.

Phone.

She needed her phone.

With laser focus, she left the porch and the railing that was supporting her, and lurched toward her car and the salvation of her phone. Her feet wouldn't work properly. She tripped over a root, or herself—she couldn't be sure—and she hit the ground on her hands and knees.

The pain ripped through her side and clouded her vision in white.

No.

She couldn't pass out. She needed to stay—

A baby's cry shattered the silence of the forest.

A baby?

Charlotte couldn't wrap her head around it. *Why would there be a baby crying in the forest?* She was hallucinating. The stress of losing Amelia and the pain...she was dying. It wasn't real.

Another cry.

Amelia.

That was real. That was Amelia's cry.

She may not have given birth to the child but she loved her in a way that couldn't be properly put into words, and she'd know that cry anywhere. Even when she was barely conscious.

Still in the dirt on her hands and knees, Char turned in the direction of the cry and forced herself to her feet. It didn't make any sense that Amelia would be crying in the forest at Lynx Creek, but it didn't have to make sense.

She needed to get to her.

That was the only thing that made sense.

It couldn't have been more than a few minutes, but it felt like hours as Charlotte stumbled and fell and made her way through the darkness toward the cries. She tripped and fell, her knees landing hard on the wooden step of the main lodge. The cries were closer now.

"Amelia. I'm coming." Her voice was barely a whisper. She was so weak. Even the pain in her side had subsided. She couldn't feel anything as she crawled into the lodge.

It wasn't until she saw Jessica, passed out next to Amelia—sitting up on a blanket next to her mother, tears running down her face—did Charlotte know for sure that she wasn't hallucinating. With all the energy she had left, Char moved to the baby and gathered her up in her blanket and held her close to her chest.

"Shh," she whispered. "I've got you."

Unable to feel her legs, Char couldn't stand. It wouldn't be safe if she fell holding the baby. So instead, she dragged herself somehow with the baby in one arm, to the far side of the cabin, where she would be out of sight if Jessica woke up or if Billy came to.

She leaned back against the wall and propped herself in such a way that she wouldn't drop Amelia. "Shh," she murmured. "It's going to be okay. It's all going to be okay. I've got you now."

In her arms, Amelia's sobbing subsided, and she wrapped her chubby fist around Charlotte's finger. It was the last thing Char remembered before losing consciousness.

Chapter Seventeen

NICK HAD TAKEN A GUESS, and he'd been right. Charlotte's car was parked outside the cabin she'd last been working on. The one where they…no. He wouldn't let himself go there. He had to focus. He was out of the vehicle and running to the door when Stephanie appeared from inside the cabin and stopped him.

"She's not in there."

"What?" He glanced around. "When did you…where is… is Amelia in…"

"No. Amelia's not—"

"And Char?"

Stephanie shook her head. "I don't know," Stephanie said. "We just got here, but—"

"We?"

"Travis is inside."

In a different circumstance, he might have let his brain process what his friend was saying, but it wasn't important. He could only focus on Charlotte and Amelia.

"What's he—"

"There's a man in there, Nick. He's unconscious and... there's a lot of—"

He pushed past her into the cabin and stopped short.

Blood. Lots of it.

Travis Bishop was crouched next to a big man, his fingers on his neck. "He has a pulse. Do you know who he is?"

Nick shook his head. "What the hell? Where is all this blood from?"

"There's a gun." Steph bent and picked it up.

"It's not from him," Travis said. "He looks like he was hit with this." He gestured to the ax lying next to the man.

Charlotte.

He looked back to the man and the spot on the floor where he'd found Charlotte upset after a phone call.

Billy.

Fuck.

Why had he let it go? When Char told him Billy had called her, that should have been enough for him to go after the man and make sure he could never get to her. He'd failed.

Nick ran a hand down his face and took a breath. He'd been too wrapped up in everything else, he'd let Charlotte get hurt. If she wasn't okay, he'd never forgive himself.

"I think this asshole is Billy," he said. "Charlotte's ex. But where is she?"

And where was Amelia?

Nick spun in a circle. "She was here." His eyes landed on the blood trail he'd stepped over in his haste to get into the cabin. So. Much. Blood. "Where is she?" A dog barked from somewhere outside, but Nick couldn't make sense of anything.

"It's Tinker Bell," Steph said. "Maybe she's found something."

Nick again looked to his friend in confusion, but Steph only grabbed his hand. "Come on. Maybe she found Char."

"I've got this," Travis said. "Go. I'll call for help."

Together, Stephanie and Nick ran through the woods. He didn't know where he was going, only that he hoped and prayed it was to Charlotte and Amelia. Somehow, he knew they were together. They had to be. But...the blood.

No.

He couldn't let himself think of the blood and what it might mean. *Was it Charlotte's? It had to be. Or...*

"This way." Steph led him over a log and toward the barking. It was getting louder.

When did Stephanie get a dog?

He couldn't think straight.

"Here."

They reached the main lodge building, where a giant puppy bounced around on the porch, barking and scratching at the closed door. Headlights shone over them as another vehicle arrived. *Damon maybe?* He didn't wait to find out. Stephanie called the dog away and Nick yanked the door open. The room was dark but with the headlights illuminating the room from outside, he could make out the shape of a woman.

"Char?"

He ran to her and dropped to his knees next to the still form, but it wasn't Charlotte. "Jessica?" She was limp, but breathing. A packet of what had to be the drugs she'd bought was on the floor next to her. He picked her up by the shoulders and shook her. Fear rose in his chest. "Jessica! Where's the baby? Where's Amelia?" He shook her again. Still no response.

Abandoning Jessica, he turned around and that's when he saw the blood. His heart sank and his entire body went numb with fear. But he forced his legs to move. To follow the blood trail around the corner.

"Char?"

She was propped up against the wall, not moving. Amelia was wrapped in a blood-stained blanket, cuddled up against Charlotte's chest, sleeping, her hand wrapped around Charlotte's finger. *And the blood. There was so much blood.* Nick dropped to his knees. His hands were everywhere and nowhere all at once. The baby, startled by the fuss, woke and immediately started crying.

"Oh thank God, Amelia." He wanted to weep with relief for his baby, but he couldn't look away from Charlotte. She wasn't moving.

"Oh my—" Katie appeared over his shoulder. "I got her." She stepped in and grabbed the baby. She whisked the baby away, and Charlotte became his only focus.

"Char." He moved her, laid her down flat on the floor, and immediately looked for a pulse. It was there. It was faint, but it was there. "Baby, no. Stay with me."

He pulled her up, so her head was cradled in his lap. "Help!" His voice cracked and hot tears burned at his eyes. "I need an ambulance."

He couldn't lose her. *Not now.*

"Stay with me, Char." He pressed his forehead to hers. "Help is coming. You're going to be okay. It's all going to be okay. Don't leave me, Char. I love you." The words slipped out with a sob. Unsure of whether she could hear him or not, he repeated them over and over until the paramedics arrived.

Chapter Eighteen

"THANK you both so much for your cooperation." The police officer, she now knew as Constable Remington Walker, who insisted on being called by his first name, led Stephanie and Travis from the examination room, where they'd been answering questions about what they'd found and how the evening had played out.

"Of course." Stephanie nodded and wrapped her arms around her waist. "Anything you need," she said. "If we can be of any more help or...well, I still can't believe he was living on the property."

"He did a good job at covering his tracks," Remington said. "He didn't want to be found. Don't beat yourself up."

Travis shook his head. "I run those trails every day. How did I not see him? I don't get it."

"Like I said," the officer said. "He was doing a pretty good job covering his tracks. He was up pretty high, past that last cabin. It looks like he'd been watching Charlotte for a while now. And, well, it all just went down at once."

"Poor Charlotte." Steph couldn't even imagine what her new friend had gone through. To be confronted by the ex who she'd fled from. How terrified she must have been. And the gunshot? "Have we heard how she is?"

Remington shook his head, as did Travis. "No new updates," he said.

"I just can't…" She sniffed back the tears that threatened and forced a smile. "Well, thank you, Officer. I feel better knowing that Billy's in custody now. And I'm sure Charlotte will…I mean…if…"

"When." Travis put his hand on her shoulder. She looked up into his eyes, softened with worry. "*When* she wakes up," he corrected.

The tenderness almost made her cry, but Stephanie swallowed back the emotion and stress of the night and managed a nod. "Right," she agreed. "*When.*"

To say the last few hours had been exciting was putting it mildly. Between the gunshot, and Billy, and then finding Jessica overdosed less than an hour after taking the baby, it was like a scene right out of one of the movies Stephanie had starred in.

She took a deep breath and looked at the two men in turn. "I guess we'll need a ride back to…" She didn't know where they should go. The idea of going back to her cabin at Lynx Creek scared her, not that she would admit it. But that man had been living on the property with her so nearby and she'd never known. The idea…well, it terrified her and made her question a lot. Maybe it wasn't such a good idea for her to be up there living on her own.

She looked at Travis and back to Remington.

"I'd like to go to the hospital," she said. "Would you mind?"

"Not at all." Remington smiled kindly.

She started walking down the hall, toward the door, when she realized Travis wasn't with her. She turned. "Are you coming?"

Travis gave the officer a look, that he clearly interpreted the way it was intended, because Remington cleared his throat and excused himself.

"I forgot that I should take care of some paperwork real quick. I'll just be a few minutes, if you two are good for a few?" He didn't wait for an answer before disappearing down the hall, back toward the offices.

When he was gone, Travis walked toward her and closed the distance.

It felt like a lifetime ago that she'd been in his arms, kissing him as if her life depended on it. And in that moment, it did.

But now…

Now he felt a million miles away, and she felt lonelier than ever before. Only worse because of what they'd experienced together.

The kiss had turned into more. And somehow they'd moved inside of Steph's cabin. His hands were hot on her bare skin and her shirt was on the floor when they'd heard the gunshot.

Would it have gone further?

Yes.

Would that have been a mistake?

She couldn't answer that.

At the time, it had felt so very right.

But now—with the way he stood just far enough away, so as not to touch her when she longed to have his arms around her, holding her; the way his lips were pressed together in a hard line instead of telling her it was all going to be okay— now, it just felt wrong.

"You don't have to come," she said before Travis could say anything. "I just feel like with everything that happened tonight I should be there for Nick and the baby and…well, I don't even know how Charlotte is and—"

"Do you want me to come?"

His voice was low, his words pointed, a challenge.

Why was everything always so hard with him?

Stephanie was exhausted. With everything. Including him.

She couldn't help the intense full-body attraction she had to him. It was aggravating and all-consuming and exciting, all at once. And then when they kissed…it was like nothing she'd ever felt before. There was a connection there that neither of them could deny. Not without lying.

Whatever was between them was real.

But…

She dropped her head and shook it slowly. "I can't do this, Travis."

"This?"

She looked up. "This…" She gestured between them. "Whatever game it is you're playing with me. The hot and cold." She took a deep breath. It had been a confusing, crazy, and mixed-up night. So many things had happened that would take some time to unwind and digest, but when she'd seen her best friend on the floor of the lodge, sobbing as the love of his life fought for her life, a few things—important things—became crystal-clear.

If she was going to risk her heart again, it would only be for someone who was willing to go all in on her. One hundred percent. Or nothing.

She shook her head. "I'm not good at games, Travis. Someone always loses."

She waited, but still, he didn't say anything. The silence was the only answer she needed. She released a long, slow breath. "I guess this time, that loser is me."

Whatever she'd been hoping for from him, she wasn't going to get it. She knew that now.

There was the strong silent type, and then there was the completely closed-off and unavailable type. Travis Bishop, in all his sexy slow smiles and smoldering eyes, was clearly the latter.

When Stephanie and Remington arrived at the hospital, the small waiting room was full. Damon sat next to Katie, who held baby Amelia. She was fast asleep, thankfully, and looked peaceful in only the way a baby who has no idea how close her life came to changing dramatically forever could. Jeremy paced at one end of the room; his parents sat together, hands clasped together, identical masks of worry on their faces. Steph had already heard from Bella, that she was on her way home to be with Jeremy and the family. She hadn't received an update on Charlotte either. Only that she was still in surgery and critical.

Natalie Collins, who'd been one of the first responders to arrive at the scene, sat with her fiancé, Aiden Adams, his arm around her, holding her close. She'd helped to stabilize Charlotte enough to move her.

She only hoped it hadn't been too late.

Her eyes scanned the room, but she didn't see Nick.

"Steph." Damon stood and offered her his seat. "Sit." He didn't wait for a response, but moved away to the corner of the room to talk to Remington, no doubt to get filled in on the rest of the situation.

"How is…" Steph sat next to Katie, who offered her a small smile. "Well, how's everyone?"

Katie chuckled a little but there was no humor in it. "This one is just fine," she said. "And that's the small blessing out of all of this. She's completely unaffected by what went on. I spoke with Susan Johnson, the caseworker, and she'll be here in the morning to assess the situation further. But we both agreed Amelia should stay with us for the night. She's had enough disruption."

Steph nodded. That seemed like a good idea. "And her—Jessica? What happened?"

Katie snorted with disgust. "An overdose." She shook her

head. "Can you believe it? She didn't even have her daughter back for a full hour before using. She's stable now, and from what we've heard…" She bent closer to Steph. "The nurses tell me that she's been going on and on about how much the baby cried and how she couldn't handle the noise." Katie sat up again. "It's disgusting. I don't know anything about anything, but I do know that Amelia should be with Nick and Charlotte."

"Well…" Steph swallowed. "I'm sure Nick is going to do everything legally he can to make that happen. And now, maybe the courts will be able to see clearly what the best thing for Amelia is."

"I hope so." Katie snuggled the baby closer. "Do you want to…"

"No." Steph shook off the offer to cuddle the little girl she thought of as a niece. "I should talk to Nick." She looked around again. "Where is he?"

Katie sighed. "Probably making the nurses crazy. He refuses to sit down. They won't let him back, and they won't tell him what's going on. All we know is she's in surgery. Still. It's probably for the best that he's not in here." Katie used her head to gesture toward Jeremy, who still hadn't sat down. "I think Jeremy might kill him if he does. I don't know why, but he's blaming Nick for all of this."

"But it was Billy."

"I know." Katie shrugged. "You can't talk to him. Either of them."

"I still can't believe this, you know?"

"I know." Katie nodded slowly. "But you know what…in a way, it's kind of good that it all played out the way it did. I mean, otherwise Charlotte wouldn't have been there. She wouldn't have heard Amelia's cries and…well, I don't want to think about it."

Steph nodded her agreement, as a question popped into her head. "How *did* she hear Amelia? I mean, the kid is loud, sure. But the lodge was a long way away from the cabin and…" She drifted off, unable to reconcile how Charlotte had heard the baby through the woods.

Katie looked down at the baby and smiled softly before looking up again. "Maybe it was motherly instinct?"

That felt right. And it was the only thing that made sense.

Stephanie bent and pressed a kiss to the little girl's head, before going in search of the baby's father.

Chapter Nineteen

IT HAD BEEN OVER AN HOUR. Almost two.

Why weren't they telling him anything? Where was the doctor? And why—

"Nick?"

He spun around so fast he almost hit Stephanie, who'd come up behind him.

"They won't tell me anything."

"I know." Her voice was gentle. "Come here." She held her arms open, but Nick shook his head.

He couldn't relax. And he definitely couldn't let himself seek comfort. Not when he didn't know whether Charlotte was going to be okay or not. She was in there because of *him*. It was his fault she was fighting for her life right now. Sure, Billy had pulled the trigger, but Charlotte never should have been there by herself. She never should have been running from him. The fact that it was his lie that made her leave, that had driven her right into Billy's trap, made him sick to his stomach.

No.

He wouldn't rest until he knew she was okay. And if she wasn't—*no!*

He wouldn't, he *couldn't* let himself think that way.

"Nick?"

"No." He shook his head. "She needs to be okay, Steph. She has to be. I can't lose her." He looked at his friend. There was nothing but kindness and understanding reflected back at him. "I love her, Steph."

"I know."

"No, you don't know. I love her," he said again. "So much. More than anything in the world. It's different with Amelia—I love her, too. But..."

"Nick?" Steph put her hand on his arm. "I know."

He stopped and looked at her. "You know?"

She nodded.

"Like you know it's not just for show? That somewhere along the way I fell for her?"

"Besides the fact that you already told me?" She grinned. "Yes. I knew. Right at the beginning," she said with a small laugh. "I think you fell for her the first time you met her. But yes, I know. I think everyone knows."

He let his lips curl up into a small smile.

"She's going to be okay, Nick. She will."

"She saved Amelia." He dropped his head, at the memory of what he'd seen. How he'd found her like that. Unconscious, with the baby protected and loved. She'd gone to her. "Can you even imagine, Steph? What it must have taken for her to go to her?"

Steph shook her head.

The police had told them that Charlotte had obviously been in the altercation with Billy at the upper cabin before making her way to the main lodge—and Amelia. "What if she hadn't have been there? What if she couldn't have gotten to her?"

"But she did."

He nodded. She did. "But how could she have—"

"Mother's instinct."

Mother's instinct?

Yes. That made sense. She was the only mother Amelia knew. And now she might not be okay. All the doctors told him was that she'd lost a lot of blood. Maybe too much.

She had to be okay. And not just for him. But for Amelia. That kind of love...that *was* a mother's love. Amelia needed Charlotte, too.

"Mr. Newton?"

Nick spun on his heel to see the doctor in a white coat with a clipboard.

"You're Ms. Davis's fiancé?"

"Yes. I am." Nick didn't hesitate. "Can I see her? Is she okay?"

Behind him, Steph murmured something about getting the rest of the family and she disappeared.

The doctor nodded slowly. "She has a long way to go," he said. "And she's lost a lot of blood. We've given her a transfusion and done surgery to repair the blood vessel and remove the bullet. She's a very lucky woman. If the bullet had been even a fraction of an inch over, it would have hit some vital organs as well, and..." The doctor shook his head. "I don't say this very often, Mr. Newton. But your fiancée, with the wound she had and the amount of blood she lost...she shouldn't have made it. It's a miracle that she pulled through."

A miracle.

It was all Nick needed to hear, but the doctor was still talking. At some point, Jeremy and Charlotte's parents arrived and were standing next to him. "She's a fighter, that's for sure," the doctor said. He repeated what he'd just said to Nick for their sake, but Nick could only focus on two words. *Pulled through.* She was going to be okay.

"She's sedated now," the doctor continued. "But you can

see her. She should be awake soon. But she'll be very tired. So keep your visits short."

He ached to see her. To hold her hand in his and tell her exactly how he felt about her. For real. Not because she was helping him out or they were just being casual, with no expectations. No. He was in absolutely, completely in love with her. With his whole body and mind. More than anything else in the world, he wanted to put his eyes on her and know for sure that she was okay.

But he needed to do something first.

"You go," Nick said to Charlotte's family. He didn't miss the way Jeremy clenched his hands into fists, and he didn't blame the man for being defensive of his sister. But he'd prove to him, to them all, that he was worthy of her. "I have something I need to do. I'll be back."

The pain was excruciating and she was so tired. But she was alive.

The last thing Charlotte remembered before passing out was holding Amelia. The baby was safe. That's all that mattered.

It was the first thing she'd asked her mother when she opened her eyes.

"Yes," Darlene said through tears. "The baby is fine. And you're fine, too. You're going to be okay, honey."

Charlotte tried to nod, but it was too much. She closed her eyes and fell back into sleep.

The next time she opened her eyes, the pain was lessened. It was more of a dull ache. Her mother was still at her side, and her dad, too. "Dad?"

"Char." He took her hand. "You gave us quite a scare, kiddo. But you're going to be okay."

They kept saying that.

"I'll kill him, Char."

Jeremy?

Her brother appeared behind her parents. "Who?" she said. "You'll kill who?"

"Billy." Jeremy spoke through gritted teeth. "If he ever gets out of jail. I'll kill him for what he did to—"

"He's alive?"

Jeremy exchanged a glance with her parents and nodded. "He is."

"I didn't…"

"No." Jeremy chuckled. "You didn't kill him. But according to the police, you knocked him pretty good. I didn't know you had it in you."

She managed a smile. "I'm pretty tough, you know?"

"We know, Char."

Was it her imagination, or was that a tear in her brother's eye?

"I'm really glad you're okay."

"We all are."

Nick.

She couldn't move quickly. Everything hurt too much, but slowly, she turned her head to the other side of the bed, and Nick.

"We'll be out in the hall, Char. We won't go far."

She didn't turn as her family made their exit. She was one hundred percent focused on the man in front of her.

He looked exhausted. His hair was rumpled on the top of his head. Behind his glasses, his eyes were rimmed in red. The scruff of a beard on his chin. If she wasn't so weak, she would have reached up and grabbed it.

As it was, it was all she could do to lift her hand and drop it back down on the bed again. "Hi."

"Hi yourself." He took her left hand in his and threaded his fingers through hers.

His touch felt so good. Instantly, she felt stronger.

"Char, I'm…I just don't know…"

She managed a small smile. "I'm okay."

"But you almost weren't." His head shot up, his eyes intense as they locked on hers. "And I don't know…well, I do know."

She blinked.

"Char, I'm so sorry I lied to you about Amelia. It's just that…I thought I could stop it. I thought I could…well, I didn't think I'd have to tell you because I didn't think it would happen and… I should have told you the truth right from the start," he finished. "I'm so sorry that I betrayed your trust like that and—"

"Shh." She held a finger to her lips. "Don't apologize anymore."

"But I need you to know that I'm sorry."

"I know." She didn't have much strength, but with the little she had, she squeezed his hand. "I know you did it for Amelia because you love her. You'd do anything for her."

He nodded.

"I know because I'd do anything for her, too."

He laughed. "You definitely demonstrated that. You almost died, Char. You lost so much blood."

"It was worth it." She meant it. She'd do it again if she had to. But she sure as hell hoped she didn't have to.

"She's safe now," Nick said, the laughter gone. "You both are. Jessica and Billy are both in custody, and I'll do everything in my power to make sure they stay that way."

He squeezed her hand again and she looked down at their fingers twined together. For the first time, she noticed the ruby ring was gone. A tear slipped from her eye.

Nick quickly wiped it away. "Char?"

"I'm okay." But she wasn't okay. Her injuries would heal. But seeing her bare finger just made her realize that it was over. All of it. There was no more need to pretend to be something she wasn't with Nick. That made her excruciatingly sad, because she wasn't pretending and hadn't been for longer than even she realized. She'd fallen in love with Nick Newton, just as hard as she'd fallen for his little girl.

"I need to tell you another secret," he continued as he unwound his hand from hers.

"There's more?" She couldn't help but try for a small smile. "I don't know if I can handle anything else."

"Well, I hope you can handle this one." He took a deep breath and pulled his shoulders back. "I'm in love with you, Charlotte Davis. Fully and completely. I think I've been in love with you from the first time I met you. I know it took me a little bit of time to—"

"What?"

"It took me a little bit of time to—"

"No." She interrupted him. "Before that." She blinked slowly. She needed to be sure she'd heard him properly and it wasn't just the drugs playing tricks with her. "You're what?"

He laughed. "I'm in love with you. Fully and completely. I may be slow to understand some things, but last night when I saw you and I thought…well, I couldn't bear it, Charlotte. I couldn't bear the idea of living this life without you. Not for one minute. I don't know what I would have done if…well, the point is, I don't want to ever know what it's like to live without you. Because I am desperately in love with you, Charlotte, and I hope to hell you feel the same way."

Fresh tears spilled unchecked down her cheeks. She nodded, but couldn't find the words to speak.

"Does that mean that—"

"I feel the same, too," she finally managed. "So much."

She sniffed and swiped at her tears, but Nick just sat there with a smile on his face. "Oh thank goodness," he said. "Because if you didn't, it would make this next question really awkward." He pulled out a ring box and flipped open the lid to reveal *the* ring.

The one she'd picked out before as the ring that would be her dream, her *real* ring. The oval emerald surrounded by tiny diamonds. The one she refused to accept unless it was for forever. She sucked in a breath as Nick started to talk.

"I've already spoken with your father and your brother." She raised an eyebrow and he laughed. "Let's just say that Jeremy and I have a few things to work out, but he wants the best for you."

"And you're the best?"

He smirked. "Hey, let me finish this, okay?"

"Okay." She closed her mouth and tried not to smile—or interrupt—while he said what he needed to say.

"Charlotte Davis, you are the kindest, most giving person I've ever met. You're braver than I ever could have imagined and the most loving, wonderful mother to Amelia. You're talented and smart and sexy as hell." He winked. "I am totally in love with every single part of you, and under no circumstances can I imagine ever wanting to spend my life without you by my side through it all. Will you please put me out of my misery and marry me for real?"

He held out the ring and she didn't hesitate.

"I thought you'd never ask."

He slid the ring on her finger, but it was the kiss he finally gave her that felt like home and promised forever.

I hope you enjoyed Nick and Charlotte's story of coming together. However, there's still one more surprise in store for this little family.

This bonus scene is exclusive to my newsletter subscribers. If you aren't hanging out with me yet, click HERE to find out what happens with Char and Nick and their extra special surprise!

It's finally time for Stephanie and Travis to come to grips with their relationship—or lack thereof. A decision to 'just be friends' simplifies things, but when a freak storm strands them together, it's not only their willpower that will be tested, but their hearts.
Cherishing Happily Ever After is next!
And read an excerpt right after this!

Cherishing Happily Ever After

Enjoy this excerpt of Cherishing Happily Ever After right after this.

WHAT WAS SHE DOING HERE?

She didn't belong.

It had been a long time since Stephanie Starz, super mega-celebrity, had felt like an outsider. A very long time.

In fact, she couldn't actually remember a time in her adult life when she'd ever felt so uncomfortable and out of place as she did at that moment. A feeling that was made even crazier considering the fact that she was surrounded by family and friends and people who loved her.

Still.

She had no business being at a Mother's Day brunch. None.

She wasn't a mother, or a stepmother, or an adopted mother, or even, for that matter, a prospective mother.

Sure, she *had* a mother. And that was the reason she'd booked the table at Birchwood. Stephanie had been so excited that her adoptive parents had finally accepted her invitation to come to Glacier Falls, the town she'd recently fallen in love with and made her hometown. She had big plans for her parents that included showing them all the sights, but mostly touring them around Lynx Creek, her newest project of a grouping of restored and renovated cabins down by the river, just outside of town, that she was getting ready to offer as exclusive bungalow retreats. And of course, Faith and Hope. Steph had been talking nonstop about her identical twin half-sisters, who she'd discovered almost by accident when she'd come to town almost a year ago to plan her own wedding.

The wedding hadn't worked out—thankfully—but she'd gained something much greater in her sisters. And all the extended family and friends she'd found in Glacier Falls. The only thing missing were her parents. Steph couldn't seem to shake the feeling that her mom and dad were avoiding her new town and coming to visit her there.

Which felt even sharper today. Mother's Day.

She'd really been looking forward to seeing them. The cancellation had come in the form of a text message the night before. *A text message.* She'd immediately picked up the phone, but her call went unanswered.

She inhaled deeply and exhaled slowly while looking around the room. Birchwood was the nicest restaurant in town —in most towns, really. Brody, the head chef and owner, was a genius and everything he created was delicious. Stephanie had eaten in some of the best restaurants in the world, and she could safely say that Birchwood was right up there with the best of them. Which was why it wasn't surprising that the place was packed.

Stephanie sipped at her tea and picked at the croissant in front of her, her face a carefully practiced mask honed from years in the spotlight. She smiled and nodded at Sarah, Brody Morris's wife, who sat in the corner close to the kitchen, where Brody could periodically pop out and join her and her daughter, Rory, for their celebration. Sarah had been a single mother for years after her first husband, Rory's father, died tragically. She deserved to be spoiled by her new husband Brody and of course her sweet daughter Rory, who was currently regaling her mother in some sort of story that involved large arm gestures.

Steph let her gaze travel to Charlotte and Nick Newton and their newly adopted daughter Amelia. Nick was one of Stephanie's best friends, and when he'd discovered that Stephanie's parents had cancelled their visit, of course he'd invited her to join them for brunch. But there was no way Steph was going to crash Charlotte's very first Mother's Day. After what they'd been through with the adoption process of Amelia, and almost losing her because the system was just so broken—never mind the fact that Amelia's birth mother was a troubled addict who'd put the baby in great danger before Charlotte scared her in a very dramatic turn of events—yes, Charlotte deserved to be celebrated today. And not only for Amelia, but for their unborn baby as well, as they'd just announced their pregnancy. Stephanie was thrilled for her friends.

Sharing a table with Nick, Charlotte, and baby Amelia were her parents, Darlene and Dwayne, and Charlotte's brother, Jeremy, along with his fiancée, Bella Burton.

Bella and Stephanie had become close friends over the last few months, working closely together on the upcoming block-buster film, *Bombshell*. The movie released next month and it was going to change Bella's world. Stephanie just knew it. Bella was going to become a massive star. But she knew her friend, and she knew that her focus was also on her relationship and her family. She wasn't going to let fame go to her head.

Bella turned, as if sensing Steph was watching her. Her pretty face turned down into a frown as she excused herself from her table and joined Steph.

"I can't stand this."

"I'm fine," Stephanie said. "I told you. I didn't want to—"

"Not you, silly girl." Bella said. "I meant this whole Mother's Day thing." She laughed and Steph joined in. "I mean, I love Jeremy's mother," she continued. "I really do. But…"

"You'd rather be with your own mom?"

Bella nodded. "Right?"

Stephanie couldn't disagree.

"Please join us," Bella said. "I can't stand seeing you sit all by yourself. It's not right."

Stephanie laughed despite the fact that there was nothing funny about it. "I actually was just going to get going," she said. "I'm not even hungry."

Bella eyed her suspiciously.

"I'm not," Stephanie insisted as she stood. She left a small stack of bills on the table even though she didn't eat anything and gathered up her purse. "Go enjoy your family. I'm just going to say good-bye to the Langdons before I head out."

"I'll call you later."

Stephanie blew her a kiss and headed over to the largest table in the room. She already knew that it was a tough day for Faith and Hope, her half-sisters, as they had lost their mother, Stephanie's birth mother, years earlier in an accident. But this Mother's Day was different because of baby Cole. Stephanie's eyes went straight to her nephew. He was only a few months old, but the sweetest baby boy she'd ever seen.

"Oh good," Hope said as she approached. "You decided to join us after all." Hope's husband, Levi, jumped up and moved to grab an extra chair, but Stephanie stopped him.

"No," she said. "I just wanted to stop by and let you know I was leaving. I have some things I need to take care of. So I'm going to get going." There was a round of protests from almost everyone, but Stephanie wouldn't be swayed. "We'll talk soon, okay?" Steph bent and gave Cole a kiss on his chubby cheek. "Be good to your mama today, kiddo."

Stephanie straightened and smoothed her signature red hair over her shoulder. "Happy Mother's Day, Mrs. Langdon." She waved across the table to Levi and Katie's mom, who'd also been like a mother to Logan, Faith's husband. "And to you, too, Katie!" She'd almost forgotten that Katie and her husband Damon were expecting their first child, too. "There's a lot to celebrate here. I hope you have a fabulous day, every-one. I'll—"

"Steph." Faith stood next to her, her hand on her arm. "Please stay and—"

"I'll pop around later, okay?" She wiggled out of her sister's grasp and managed to escape out into the warm spring day, where she could finally take a breath.

She truly loved everyone inside, and it didn't usually bother her that she was single and alone. But for some reason, her singleness was becoming harder and harder to ignore when all around her, the people she loved were all getting their happily ever afters while she…well, she just couldn't seem to figure out her own happy ending.

"Tink!" Travis Bishop pulled his T-shirt over and off his head and used it to wipe his forehead before he popped his cowboy hat back on. "Tinker Bell! Leave that alone." He called the puppy away from his pile of wood, where she was trying to pull a board off the neat stack. He'd adopted the puppy almost two months earlier, or more accurately, she'd adopted him when he'd found her in the woods, lying in a patch of crocuses, lost, cold, and hungry. After a bit of digging, he'd learned that a litter of puppies had been abandoned down the road and most of the other pups had been rounded up and taken to the shelter. The animal control officer told him he was welcome to surrender her to the shelter as well. A kill shelter.

No way.

He may not be a softie, but he wasn't totally dead inside. Besides, she'd obviously been spunky enough to wander away from her litter mates in search of food and shelter. If she was independent enough to do that, she wouldn't be too needy for him. At least, that was the theory. It hadn't taken long for Tinker Bell, named because he liked the irony of a dainty name for what was likely to be a massive dog, to wiggle her way into Travis's heart.

He was used to being alone. Preferred it, really. But the puppy's companionship wasn't offensive. Even if she was a pain in the ass from time to time. "Tink! I said, leave it."

With a growl, the puppy managed to pull a board from the pile, causing the whole thing to topple over, scaring her. She whimpered and ran to Travis to hide behind his legs. "Silly dog." He bent down to reassure her and rough up her fur. A moment later, the puppy was licking his hand and jumping at his face, the scare forgotten.

"Come on. We're never going to get this done at this rate."

Once more, Travis picked up his hammer, grabbed a board from the stack, and set to work on the fence he'd been working on. It was a simple perimeter fence, and although it wouldn't serve to keep anything or anyone out if they really wanted into the property at Lynx Creek, it would serve as a border marker for the security system he'd ordered for Stephanie Starz's property. He hadn't told her yet about the state-of-the-art system he'd picked out for her, but he had a feeling she wasn't going to disagree with him that it was a good idea. She'd been pretty shaken by the incident that had taken place in her cabins less than six weeks ago.

As had he.

Shaken maybe wasn't the right word.

More like angry. *Really* angry.

It's not as though it were his job to defend the property from intruders. He'd been hired to fix up the cabins, build decks, and generally fix things. Not protect them.

Still.

The fact that he'd been living so close by and hadn't noticed that a strange man—who'd turned out to be the abusive ex-boyfriend of a local woman, Charlotte—had been living on the land and stalking Charlotte for weeks before making himself known in what had culminated in a very dramatic series of events that had left Charlotte with a gunshot wound she'd almost died from, didn't sit well with Travis. Not at all.

How hadn't he noticed the man? What would have happened if he'd come across Stephanie? Steph had been staying in her cabin, down by the river. Alone. She would have been defenseless by herself.

It wasn't Travis's fault that it had happened, but it didn't mean he didn't blame himself at least a little—or a lot. It also didn't mean that he couldn't do something about it now.

Which was why he was building the fence. It was something. Even if it wasn't enough. Stephanie hadn't stayed in the cabin since it had all happened. She hadn't come right out and said anything, but Travis knew she was scared. And he hated it.

He'd been with Stephanie in her cabin the night everything happened. They'd been...well...he'd been consoling her.

With her shirt off and his hands—

Who knew how things would have turned out if they hadn't heard the gunshot?

He knew.

He knew how it would have turned out. He'd wanted Stephanie almost from the moment he'd laid eyes on her, and he was pretty sure the feeling was completely reciprocated. He knew exactly how the rest of the night would have gone.

He'd found her crying and lonely. So he'd wrapped an arm around her and then finally let himself do what he'd been trying not to for months. He'd kissed her and it had been… everything. Once they'd gone inside and clothes had started to come off, Travis knew exactly what would have happened. He would have taken her to bed and shown her exactly how she made him feel. And it was anything but lonely.

The gunshot had interrupted them, and he'd spent the last few weeks feeling conflicted about that interruption.

It was for the best. He didn't do relationships. Not of any kind. And especially not with a woman like Stephanie Starz. He did casual, no strings attached, one-night stands with zero expectations. Period. End of story.

Except…

The slam of a car door yanked him from his thoughts. Before he could call her back, Tinker Bell barked and took off running in the direction of the new arrival. With a sigh, he dropped the hammer and set after the dog. "Tink! Come!"

Shit. He really was going to have to start working on some basic training with the puppy before she—

He stopped at the edge of the trees before stepping out into the clearing, frozen by the sight of the familiar red hair. Stephanie sat in the dirt next to her car, the puppy between her legs trying desperately to climb all over her and lick her face.

Travis couldn't keep himself from smiling when he heard her sweet laughter.

Okay. Maybe he didn't need to work on too much training.

"Hey there."

The sweet sound of Stephanie's laughter died abruptly when she heard his voice. She pulled herself up from the dirt, brushed off her clothes, and crossed her arms over her chest. "I didn't expect you to be here."

What was Travis doing there? She'd come to Lynx Creek because it was her safe place. Her place where she could just turn off the rest of the world and just...*be.*

At least, it had been that place.

After the incident with Charlotte's ex and the shooting and the blood...*the blood*... Never mind what could have gone wrong that night. *Could have.* But it didn't go wrong. Charlotte was okay. The baby was okay. Everyone was okay.

Everybody but her.

Stephanie didn't want to admit it, especially to herself, but that night had affected her more than she'd thought it would. Lynx Creek didn't seem like her peaceful, safe sanctuary anymore. And she hated it.

"Long time no see."

She took a step back from him. It was a defense mechanism. She couldn't be close to him. Not without wanting to touch him. Or worse, kiss him. And really, would it *kill* him to put a shirt on?

"I've been busy." Stephanie shrugged. "Spending a lot of time in the city getting ready for the new movie. There hasn't been a lot of time to get out here and...check on things."

He arched an eyebrow and his lips quirked up into a cocky grin that sparked a heat low in her belly. Steph had to bite back a sharp retort and the groan of frustration that bubbled up inside her. Travis always had this effect on her. This love-hate thing that made her both want to scream and laugh. Run away or throw herself into his arms. And... "Do you not *own* any shirts?"

His grin got wider, and she was instantly annoyed with herself for saying anything at all. For *noticing*.

"I do."

She took another step back. "And why is it you don't actually wear any?" She needed to stop talking about his half-nakedness. It shouldn't bother her. It shouldn't even affect her. After all, who cared if he didn't wear clothes at all? She didn't.

Not true.

She cared.

A lot.

Travis had muscles that she didn't even know existed on a man. There was literally no part of him that wasn't lean and ripped. But not in a muscle-bound, bulky, and hard way. No. Travis was built like a man who'd spent his life working hard for what he had. His body was not built in the gym. It was one hundred percent built from his life and the hard work he'd done to have that life. Steph had stared across Hollywood's hottest and sexiest stars. She'd seen many of them almost completely naked and had her share of love scenes with some of the world's most desirable and eligible bachelors. She was no stranger to being surrounded by beautiful people. But Travis...

She swallowed hard.

"Does it bother you?"

He was so cocky it made her want to scream. He knew damn well it bothered her. *He* bothered her. The hot-and-cold, cat-and-mouse game he'd been playing with her almost from the moment they met bothered her.

Stephanie shook her head and crouched down to pet the dog, who was biting at her shoes. "Do what you need to do." She scratched behind Tink's ears. "What *are* you doing here anyway?" She looked up without standing. "I thought your work here was done."

In fact, she *knew* it was done. He'd sent her a final invoice less than two weeks ago. After the incident, when she'd gone back to the city, he'd put the final push on finishing up the cabins and cleaning up any traces of what had happened. Not that she'd checked. But as annoying as Travis could be, he was also a quality worker and a very talented craftsman. She trusted him.

"Did you check it out?"

She shook her head.

"Would you like me to show you?"

She shook her head again and the smile slipped from his face.

Travis took a step toward her. "Is that because you're scared to be back here or you're scared of me?"

White-hot anger flashed through her. Steph stood so abruptly, Tink jumped back and out of her way. "What makes you think I'm scared?"

"Of this place? Or of me?"

"I'm not scared of you."

"But you *are* scared of Lynx Creek?"

She swallowed hard. She would *not* answer that.

"I get it, Steph."

His voice was low, maybe even caring. But she couldn't trust him. She'd done that once before. She'd let her guard down with him only once, but it was long enough to learn that it was a bad idea. A *really* bad idea. She wouldn't do it again.

She shook her head and put a smile on her face. She was a damn good actress, and she'd prove it. "I'm not scared of Lynx Creek." She flipped her hair over her shoulder and turned to walk down toward the river. "I wouldn't have bought it if I was scared of it."

She was done with Travis Bishop.

Dealing with him was the last thing she needed today after a disastrous brunch. All she really needed was to sit by the river for a few minutes, listen to the birds, and try to forget that the one place in the world that had made her feel like she was part of something now felt foreign and unsure. The last thing Stephanie needed was Travis pointing it out to her.

No, thank-you.

She'd gotten halfway down the trail that would take her to the river when Travis called out behind her.

"Stephanie?"

Something in his voice stopped her. It wasn't his usual cockiness and self-assuredness. This was different. He sounded…sincere. She turned around slowly.

"There really is something I'd like to show you." He held his hand out. "I think you're going to like it."

Travis didn't expect her to come with him. Not really. And he wouldn't have blamed her if she didn't. He'd been…well, he'd been confused when it came to her.

Confused.

That was a piece of shit, copout explanation when it came to Stephanie. He was a lot of things, but *confused* about how he felt about Stephanie Starz was not one of them.

She stared at his outstretched hand but curiosity ultimately won out and to his surprise, and pleasure, she nodded once and walked past him and his hand. "Fine."

Travis shook his head with a grin and tucked his hand into his back pocket. It was a small victory and he'd take it. For now.

She followed as Travis led the short way through the woods to the worksite where he'd left his tools and his shirt. He grabbed it and tugged it over his head.

Was that a flash of disappointment he saw in her eyes?

"Getting cold?" She was so naturally sweet that even when she tried to be sarcastic, it still came off as cute. Travis couldn't help but smile as she stood with her arms crossed, trying—and failing—to look tough and unaffected.

"I thought you might…" He cocked his head at her, but she only widened her eyes in response. He shook his head and tried again. "I'm getting a little chilly." It was a warm day, but he didn't want to argue with her anymore. Quite the opposite.

"What did you want to show me?"

Travis stepped back and waved an arm behind him. "This."

He watched as she looked at the fence she hadn't noticed when they'd first arrived at the site. She took a step closer and her eyes widened in question. She looked down the length of the fence line and he knew what she'd seen there. He'd been working hard. It was almost done. Slowly, she looked back at him. "What is…a fence?"

Travis nodded. "It goes around the entire perimeter of the property," he said. "Well, almost. There are still a few gaps I need to close up."

"But…I didn't ask—"

"I know." He held up a hand to ward off the objections he was sure would be coming next. "You didn't ask me to do it," he said. "And you don't need to pay me for it. It's a gift."

"A gift?"

He nodded. "I know you were a little…well, after everything went down up here with Char and…" He wasn't getting this right. "I know you haven't been feeling very comfortable up here since it all happened. And I don't—"

"I'm not uncomfortable. I told you, I've been—"

"Busy," he finished for her. "I know, you said."

He held her gaze for a moment and could see the truth reflected in the depths of her emerald-green eyes. She looked away first and stepped toward the fence. She ran her hand along the top piece of wood. It was a simple style. Rustic, to match the entire aesthetic of Lynx Creek, he'd made sure that it wouldn't stick out.

"It's…but I don't understand. It doesn't look like it will keep anyone out." She turned and looked at him quickly. "Not that I thought that's what you—"

"It won't keep animals out either." He cut her off. "That's not what I built it for." She looked confused, so he continued quickly. "In this part of the mountains, you don't want to keep all the wildlife out because Lynx Creek is in the middle of a wildlife corridor. If you built anything to obstruct that, it would cause issues with migration and breeding and…well, it's not good."

She nodded.

"Besides, if you really wanted to keep everything out, it would be a twenty-foot-high fence and on a property this size…" He trailed off when he saw the way she looked at him.

"So if it's not built to keep anyone—I mean, anything—out, then why?"

He nodded and grinned. "It's a perimeter for the security system I found for you. You set it up along the fence line and then adjust the settings for the environment. So for example, we should be able to adjust for wildlife so they can still cross the property unrestricted. But you'll get an alert if any…non-wildlife crosses the perimeter. And you can even set it so if there is an issue with bears or wolves, you, or whomever is the caretaker of the property, will be alerted and can keep an eye out. For safety."

She nodded as what he said sank in. "For safety."

"Exactly."

She looked at the fence intently. "And we'll be alerted if bears or people cross the perimeter?"

He nodded. She was trying so hard to prove she wasn't scared to be at Lynx Creek. Her stubbornness was cute. Very cute. And if it made her feel better and more in control, he'd happily play along. "We can even set it so that the conservation officers or police are alerted immediately as well. It's a pretty sophisticated system."

She nodded thoughtfully and finally turned to him. "That

does sound sophisticated and it'll be good to have that level of protection. For…for the guests."

"Of course."

She smiled knowingly, the first genuine smile he'd gotten from her all afternoon. It was gorgeous and it warmed him in a way that had him wanting to remove more than just his T-shirt. "You just did this? Without asking or—"

"Like I said…" He held out a hand. "You don't have to pay me. I know I should have asked you about it before starting, but I wanted to…" He blew out a breath and decided to go with honesty. "I wanted to surprise you, Steph. I thought maybe if you had a bit of security, you would…well, maybe you'd feel better about staying here again."

Travis watched myriad emotions play out over her face.

"So you did this…for me?"

He nodded and took a step toward her. He longed to touch her. To take her face in his hand and hold her there so he could press his lips to hers again. It was pretty much the only thing he'd thought about for the last six weeks. Holding her. Kissing her. Laying her down.

Travis knew it was trouble. Stephanie wasn't the type of woman who went in for no strings attached, uncomplicated and easy.

But he'd tried to stay away. For months. She was like a magnet pulling him in.

"I don't really know what to say." Stephanie's tongue slipped out between her lips and she bit her bottom lip.

He couldn't stop himself. He reached for her but she took a step back and shook her head quickly. "No."

"No?"

She shook her head again. "I don't play games, Travis." She turned to go, and suddenly he was desperate to keep her there.

"We're already playing, Steph."

They *had* been playing. For months. A game of cat-and-mouse, push and pull. They got closer and then someone pulled away. She might say she didn't want to play games, but as far as Travis was concerned, it was too late for that.

She froze and shook her head before she turned around and looked him straight in the eye. "I already told you, Travis. When it comes to games, there's always a loser. And that's not going to be me. Not anymore." She looked down for a moment and then added, "Thank you for the fence."

Read the rest of Travis and Stephanie's story in Cherishing Happily Ever After next.

About the Author

Elena Aitken is a USA Today Bestselling Author of more than forty romance and women's fiction novels. Living a stone's throw from the Rocky Mountains with her teenager twins, their two cats and a goofy rescue dog, Elena escapes into the mountains whenever life allows. She can often be found with her toes in the lake and a glass of wine in her hand, dreaming up her next book and working on her own happily ever after with her very own mountain man.

To learn more about Elena:
www.elenaaitken.com
elena@elenaaitken.com

www.ingramcontent.com/pod-product-compliance
Lightning Source LLC
Chambersburg PA
CBHW022141240626
47153CB00007B/2451